Wanton in Winter

The Wicked Winters Book Three

BY
SCARLETT SCOTT

Wanton in Winter
The Wicked Winters Book Three

ISBN: 978-1-706129-23-3

Edited by Grace Bradley
Cover Design by Wicked Smart Designs

For more information, contact author Scarlett Scott.
www.scarlettscottauthor.com

Cameron Blythe, the Earl of Hertford, is about to lose nearly everything he owns to creditors in the wake of his blackguard father's death. The only way to stave off ruin is to find a wealthy wife, even if it means aligning himself with one of the infamous Winter sisters. Any of the chits will do. Except for Miss Eugenia Winter, that is, whose reputation has been tainted by scurrilous gossip.

When Eugie spurned an odious, fortune-hunting suitor, the last thing she expected was for him to spread shocking lies about her. Determined to stop her beloved sisters from falling prey to a similar, painful fate, she will do anything to keep the penniless Earl of Hertford from making a match with one of them. Even if it means cornering him in a darkened winter's garden and kissing him herself.

But when one kiss turns into another, and then another, the strictly proper Cam cannot help himself from falling for the Winter with the most wicked reputation of all. And Eugie? Much to her dismay, she's discovering the irresistible earl may be everything she has ever wanted. Does she dare trust her heart, or will the painful lessons of her past prove too impossible to overcome?

Dedication

*For my readers, with more gratitude
than I can put into words.*

Chapter One

Oxfordshire, 1813

"*I* FEEL LIKE a damned Michaelmas goose," Cameron Blythe, the Earl of Hertford, muttered, *sotto voce.*

At his side, Rand, Viscount Aylesford, chuckled. "Perhaps you can convince one of the chits that marrying you will be good luck, much like eating the goose."

Cam surveyed the ballroom before them. Lit with at least a dozen chandeliers, it was a study in festive gaiety. Lady Emilia Winter and her husband Mr. Devereaux Winter were celebrating the pending Christmas season in a fashion befitting their tremendous wealth.

And also befitting a man who had five unmarried sisters he needed to settle with husbands. Title hunters, all of them, Cam was sure.

"Succumbing to the parson's mousetrap is only one breed of luck, Aylesford, and it is decidedly not good," he ventured, unable to keep the bitterness from his tone.

"Truth, which is why I have no intention of doing it myself." Aylesford brushed at the sleeve of his coat, affecting *ennui* as few others could. "Ingenious of you to suggest a false engagement. It should be just the thing to convince the dowager I have reformed my rakish ways."

Cam tried to envision the august dowager Duchess of Revelstoke uttering the word *rakish* and failed. "The dowager would refuse to lower herself by saying such a word on principle."

Aylesford sighed. "You are right, of course. Your indefatigable sense of propriety is why she loves you. Pity you could not have been born her grandson instead of I."

Though a longtime friend of Cam's, Aylesford was undeniably a rakehell possessed of a reputation to compete with Beelzebub himself. "The notion of what is proper was beaten into me from an early age by my wastrel sire."

His tone was mild, but the sentiment behind it was decidedly not. His father had been a ruthless tyrant who enjoyed inflicting pain on his family almost as much as he enjoyed gambling. As it stood now, Cam would have preferred additional beatings to the financial wreckage he had inherited from the former earl.

Creditors hounding him everywhere. Estates on the brink of ruin. A darling mother he could not bear to see tossed into the streets after all she had endured. There was only one solution to the endless list of his worries, and it was finding himself an heiress and making her his countess.

With all haste.

"Pity the old earl is dead," Aylesford drawled. "Had I an inkling of what he was about, I would have delivered him the drubbing he deserved before he stuck his spoon in the wall. If anyone ought to have his resting place ransacked by grave robbers, it is your father."

Cam flinched, although it was true. "There was nothing to be done. The money was his to spend, the estates his to fleece as he liked. Just as my mother was his to beat until I was big enough to defend her."

"Any man who would beat a woman ought to be horsewhipped himself," his friend said somberly. "One can only hope he is receiving his true reward for a life of inflicting misery on everyone he knew and is roasting in the fieriest coals of hell as we speak."

Talk of graves and the pits of hell were creating a decidedly dampening effect upon Cam's desire to dance with a lady.

"You are a grim one tonight, Aylesford," he observed.

The viscount grinned back at him, unrepentant. "I am all manner of things I ought not to be. But hopefully one of them is a man who is not being harangued by his dowager grandmother to wed. That she is withholding Tyre Abbey from me until I am betrothed is out of bounds."

Tyre Abbey was a wealthy estate in Scotland, belonging to the dowager in her own right. And though an understanding had always existed that Aylesford would one day take possession of the property, the dowager was wisely dangling it over her grandson's head in an effort to get him to do what she wanted.

"Nothing like familial bribery to warm the heart," he quipped, for in truth, he did rather enjoy the dowager, if not her attempts to wreak havoc upon his friend's bachelor ways.

"You like the old bird better than anyone," Aylesford said. "Do you think my sham betrothal strategy will work?"

"As long as you can find the proper pretend-betrothed to agree to the farce, you ought to be able to buy yourself at least a year of freedom," he reassured his friend. "Her Grace will be so pleased at the prospect of a reformed Aylesford, it will take her some time to realize the betrothal is becoming a lengthy one. I, on the other hand, will not be nearly as fortunate since my betrothal will necessarily be followed by the actual deed."

He suppressed a shiver at the thought of the manner in which he was being forced to sell himself. *For Mother*, he reminded himself. He would do anything for her, just as she had once protected him from the fists of his father.

Aylesford sipped his punch, casting his eye about the

lively gathering—presumably for his quarry. "Who shall I choose, I wonder? One of the Winters ought to do. Rumor has it Devereaux Winter is quite desperate to see them wed and off his hands, but the ladies are not as eager."

Cam's gaze followed his friend's to where the five Winter sisters had gathered, rather reminiscent of a battle formation. They were lovely, which somewhat aided in removing the stench of trade surrounding them.

Their father had been a wealthy merchant, but their brother had turned their family fortune into an empire. Though they had been doing their utmost to buy *entrée* into society, it had only been Winter's marriage to Lady Emilia King—coupled with the immense dowries each sister reportedly possessed—that made the thought of marrying them palatable for Cam.

All of them except for the one with the bad reputation, that was.

"Not the one in the red gown," he said. "She possesses the worst reputation of the lot. Baron Cunningham claims she allowed him to anticipate the wedding night. When he discovered he was not her first conquest, he cried off immediately. The dowager will never accept her."

"Cunningham is an ass," Aylesford observed thoughtfully. "And also a notorious liar."

Cam found his gaze lingering upon Miss Eugenia Winter. Her curves were lovingly revealed by the scarlet net evening dress. Embroidery around the décolletage emphasized her plump bosom, as if intentionally drawing the masculine eye to that wicked place. He could not deny the allure of her creamy breasts or the flare of her hips. Or her mouth, which seemed far too wide and lush even from across the room.

Indeed, everything about her looked like an invitation to sin.

Cam tore his stare from her and settled it back upon his friend. "Cunningham may be an ass and a liar, but all one needs to do is take a look at Miss Eugenia Winter to know she is every bit as immoral as her reputation suggests. Just look at her in that dress."

"I am looking," Aylesford said on a grin. "I fail to see the issue with an immoral woman. I have kept company with— and heartily appreciated—legions of them."

Cam snorted. "I have no doubt of that. But you must keep in mind you are not seeking your next mistress, Aylesford. You are seeking a betrothed to keep the dragon dowager from breathing fire at you for the next year. She will not approve of that one's reputation."

"She will not approve of any of them, truth be told." Aylesford's sigh was steeped in resentment. "But that is too bad. My odds are one in five. Any of them will do."

That was rather the attitude Cam had adopted in relation to the Winter sisters. His debt was colossal. Only a sickeningly wealthy bride would save him from ruin.

Except for the red gown, he reminded himself. He would sooner be cast into penury than accept the tainted leavings of an oaf like Cunningham. Wealth and reasonable respectability. In that order.

EUGIE USED HER fan to great advantage, shielding her lips as she spoke to her sister, Grace. "Would you look at the two of them? They are eying us as if we are, the five of us, about to be auctioned off at Tattersall's."

Grace flapped her own fan, her expression one of keen boredom. "Preening peacocks. Little do they know, we have no intention of accepting a proposal from anyone. 'Tis almost sad, really. I would feel sorry for them if they were not such pompous hypocrites."

"But they are, judging us for our father, our brother, for our wealth and our reputations," Eugie agreed, her gaze slipping back to the tall man with the light-brown hair, the slashing jaw, and expression of extreme disapproval.

He was handsome, arrestingly so, and even from a distance. Which aggrieved her mightily, for she knew he was no different than any of his fellow lordling counterparts. The stains upon her reputation would never be lifted, and neither would the scars upon her heart.

She would do anything, *anything* to keep her beloved sisters from suffering a fate similar to the one she had. For a time, she had fancied herself in love with Lord Cunningham, and she had truly believed he had loved her in return. Until she had discovered the awful truth, and he had turned against her in spectacular fashion, spreading gossip and lies so putrid they did not bear repeating.

"Your reputation should never have been called into question by that spineless, sniveling fool," Grace snapped, waving her fan. "Dev should have shot him when he had the chance."

"It is better for us all that he did not, and you know it," she told her sister.

Their protective and beloved older brother, Dev, had wanted to challenge Cunningham to a duel. Eugie had begged him not to. Better to lose her honor than to lose the man who held their family together. She had been right—her brother's intense devotion to all his sisters had precluded him from taking the chance he would be removed from their lives forever. The duel had not been fought. Cunningham had continued to spread his lies.

Oh, Dev had made his life a misery in the last few

months, buying up his debts in preparation for a true reckoning, but the damage had already been inflicted by his lies. Eugie was damaged goods. Dev could pretend she was not. Her sister-in-law, Lady Emilia could invite every eligible *parti* in the realm to this blasted country house party.

Nothing would change the fact that everyone in this ballroom believed she had allowed the horrid Lord Cunningham liberties she ought to have reserved for her husband.

"Dev would have won," Grace insisted. "Oh dear Lord, here they come with our own brother."

"*Et tu, Brute?*" Eugie muttered at the sight of her brother and sister-in-law leading the two lords in their direction.

"At least they are handsome," chimed in their sister, Christabella. "And I have heard wicked things about Lord Aylesford. He is a *rake*."

Eugie sent a disapproving frown in Christabella's direction. "Do stop reading Minerva Press novels, sister. Rakes do not a good husband make."

"Nor do barons," Christabella shot back.

"That was an unbecoming taunt," Grace informed their sister from the corner of her mouth as Dev and his coterie drew nearer.

"She is right, however," Eugie admitted. "If I can spare you all the pain I suffered, I would experience it again a hundredfold."

"No need to be a martyr," said Pru, the eldest—and, by chance—tallest of her sisters. "We are all aware that many lords are snakes in sheep's clothing."

"Gads. It is a wolf," Grace drawled, waving her fan in a more pronounced fashion, as though her presence at the ball bored her.

"What is a wolf?" Eugie asked, quite lost, as was often the case when one was attempting to converse with four sisters at once. Speaking of which, where had her youngest sister gone? "Where is Bea?"

No one said a word.

"A wolf in sheep's clothing," Grace added. "You had it all wrong, Pru."

In the next moment, the approaching storm had reached them. Both the lords in question—the Earl of Hertford and Viscount Aylesford—were strikingly handsome. They were near enough now, Eugie could see all the details escaping her from across the chamber.

The Earl of Hertford was the man with the jaw and the light-brown hair and the mouth, Lord in heaven *the mouth*, and the disapproving hazel stare that raked over Eugie in far too familiar a fashion.

Stopping upon her bosom.

It was not the first such look she had received, and nor would it be the last, she knew. She frowned at him as her heart thumped with a steadily increasing rhythm. *Stupid heart.* It had proven itself untrustworthy.

Dev was saying something, and since he was her brother, Eugie had ignored most of it. Only the last few words reached her ears.

"…delighted."

Very well, only the last word, quite specifically. Which did her not one whit of good.

Because everyone was staring at her expectantly.

She blinked. That hazel gaze was upon her with the weight of an anvil.

"The next dance," Lord Hertford was saying.

To her.

Eugie blinked. Oh dear, what else had she missed? And had Dev truly just promised she would dance with the Earl of Hertford? She had been so caught up in her thoughts, she had not heard the majority of the discourse happening around her.

Grace was accepting Lord Aylesford's arm.

Eugie frowned at her, sending her a look that said *what are you doing?*

Grace shrugged, returning an expression that said *I have no idea, but I am bored.*

Drat Grace. And drat Dev for introducing them to these detestable lords, for harboring this nonsensical idea he could give their family name some respectability if they all wedded a lord just as he had married a lady.

The earl offered her his arm.

She glanced to Christabella, who was notoriously abysmal at hiding her emotions, and whose expression was a mask of pity. Instantly, she looked to her brother's wife, Lady Emilia, who rolled her lips inward, her brows furrowing as she met Eugie's gaze with a beseeching look of her own.

Forgive me, it said.

"The dance is beginning," Dev prodded her. "You will not wish to miss it."

"Miss Winter," the earl said formally, his tone cool. Cold, even.

He, too, was privy to the rumors. She knew it in her gut the way she knew winter was descending upon them, the way she knew Christmas was a few weeks hence.

Of course, he was aware of the vile lies being spread about her. Was not everyone in all London? She knew, instinctively, that Dev had somehow cleverly maneuvered the earl into offering to dance with her.

And also that the earl was decidedly not so inclined.

But he had accepted, in spite of himself.

"Eugie," her brother prodded then, "the dance will begin at any second. You do not wish to tarry, do you?"

Eugie's lips compressed, and she did not miss the look her

sister-in-law sent in her brother's direction. But she would save him, just as she would save them all.

She placed her gloved hand on Lord Hertford's proffered arm, and she allowed him to lead her away from her siblings. The heat of him seeped through her gloves, irking her, as did the remarkably firm sensation of his well-muscled arm beneath hers.

Perhaps he was a gentleman who had taken to boxing, or some other means of physical toil, for Lord Cunningham had certainly never been so firm. Never so strong. Nor had he been so handsome, and while Lord Hertford smelled deliciously of shaving soap, man, and leather, Cunningham had smelled of pipe smoke and hair wax.

She should have taken heed of such a sign before it had been too late.

"Thank you for paying me the honor of this dance, Miss Winter," the earl said stiffly as they approached the dancers forming in lines on the polished parquet of the dance floor.

How formal he was. How joyless. She disliked his mannerisms every bit as much as she loathed her unwanted reaction to him. He was not, after all, the first handsome man she had ever seen. And she was weary of gentlemen looking upon her sisters as if they were purses of gold rather than ladies with hearts and minds.

The final thread holding her patience in place broke. "Why are you dancing with me when you so plainly have no wish to do so, my lord?" she demanded, piqued.

"Who says I have no wish to do so?" he asked softly, his tone still formal.

"Your countenance," she returned, forcing a bright smile to her lips. "It speaks for you, Lord Hertford."

He arched a brow and sent a quelling look in her direction. "And what is it saying now, Miss Winter?"

She stared back at him, a surge of defiance making her bold. "It is saying you are a pompous bore."

A *handsome*, pompous bore.

His lips twitched, almost as if he were about to laugh. "Perhaps I might return your question to you. Why are *you* dancing with me when it seems you have no wish to do so, Miss Winter?"

But there was the problem. She rather *did* want to dance with him, and she did not like the urge. Thankfully, she was saved from having to answer when they took their positions in the lines, opposite each other. Their gazes met and held, and she could not help but to read a challenge in his. She inclined her head in acknowledgment.

The orchestra struck up a lively reel in the next instant, and the time for talking was done.

Chapter Two

" *I* THINK I shall ask the chit in the red dress after all, in spite of her somewhat sullied reputation," Aylesford told Cam the next morning as their mounts trotted beside each other in the sprawling park of Abingdon Hall.

For reasons he did not care to examine, the proclamation disturbed Cam. He found himself frowning into the frost-kissed grass undulating before them, then beyond to the tree-lined horizon. "Miss Eugenia Winter," he said.

Eugie, Mr. Winter had called her, and the diminutive suited her far better than Eugenia did. The name Eugie had a sweetness to it, like a confection one could not help but devour. Fitting, he thought. She was soft and lush, curves everywhere a man could want, and when he had danced with her the night before, he had realized she was prettier at proximity than she had been from afar.

Even if she had gazed upon him as if he were a thief she had caught in the act of filching the family silver. Most vexing, that. What had she to disapprove of in him? He was the Earl of Hertford. Even drowning in debt, he was a catch. Whilst she was decidedly the opposite.

"That is the one," Aylesford said cheerily. "If I am to have a betrothed, I have decided I should like one who is not averse to a spot of fun, now and again."

He clenched his jaw. Of all the Winter sisters, Eugie

seemed designed, by the Lord Himself, for just the sort of fun Aylesford referred to. Her berry-red lips were a perpetual pout a man could not help but want to kiss. Her breasts would more than fill his hands. And her chocolate-brown eyes…

Dear God, what was he waxing on about? Had the unseasonably cold December air infected his mind? Surely it had. That was the only reason to find his thoughts lingering upon such an unsuitable female. He had come to Abingdon Hall to secure himself a bride and a fortune, not to lust over the Winter with the most scandal-tainted reputation.

"Here now, Aylesford," he still felt compelled to admonish, "when I proposed the idea of you taking on a counterfeit fiancée, I never intended for you to seduce the girl. Whoever she is, you must leave her just as she was upon entering into the arrangement when you sever it."

Especially if you choose Miss Eugie Winter, said a voice inside him.

Aylesford, however, was undeterred by his censure. He grinned. "I said fun, old chap. What is the harm in a few kisses, here or there? Perhaps a chance encounter in the garden?"

"No," he bit out before he could rein himself in or wonder why the notion of Aylesford stealing away with Eugie Winter into the garden might fill him with a possessive surge of protection.

Protection? For a female who had not smiled at him once as they shared a dance, and who had already thoroughly ruined herself?

How foolish.

How mutton-headed.

Aylesford was eying him with a knowing look. "You want the red dress for yourself, do you?"

"Cease referring to her as that, will you?" he grumbled in

spite of himself. "She has a name."

"Ah, yes. Euphemia, was it?" his friend asked.

He compressed his lips, refusing to accept Aylesford's bait. "You damn well know what it is."

"Forgive me, Hertford," the viscount drawled. "I had not realized you had settled upon her *yourself*. Perhaps I shall take the sister who was standing beside her, the lovely one who looked at me as if I were an unavoidable mud puddle. Her breasts are not as large as your future countess's, but as they say, any more than a handful is a waste."

Cam reminded himself to aim for Aylesford's eye the next time they were sparring together at Grey's Boxing Salon. "You have it all wrong. I am not about to offer for Miss Eugie. Her reputation speaks for itself."

"As does her figure," his friend added with a wicked grin. "If Cunningham truly did get beneath her skirts, he was a fortunate man indeed."

"You will never fool the dowager into believing you are a reformed man with this sort of attitude," he felt compelled to point out, aware he sounded as if his valet had tied his cravat too tightly that morning.

"Fortunately for me, you are not my grandmother." Aylesford winked at him. "But you do sound rather a lot like the old bird, the more I think on it. Little wonder they call you the Prince of Proper."

"Go to hell, Aylesford," he told his friend before spurring his mount into a gallop. With the bracing winter wind against his cheeks, he headed for the horizon, putting some much-needed distance between himself and the taunting laughter of his friend.

THERE WAS SOMETHING about the Earl of Hertford that made Eugie incredibly suspicious of him. Gathering her pelisse about her to stave off the chilly nip of the wind, she turned a corner in the gardens, rounding a beautifully manicured wall of holly.

One of the loveliest aspects of the Abingdon Hall grounds—to her mind, at least—was not the immense limestone edifice with its two hundred rooms and picture gallery and entry hall large enough to house an entire London tenement. Rather, it was the massive amount of outdoor space. Having been born and raised in the city, Eugie appreciated nature, even in its frozen, wintry state. The lack of buildings, the absence of sound, the beauty of the land and vegetation, held her in their thrall.

But not so much that she forgot the task at hand. Namely, deciphering which of her sisters the Earl of Hertford and his ne'er-do-well friend, Viscount Aylesford, had settled upon as matrimonial prospects.

After what had happened with Baron Cunningham, Eugie was no longer the naïve girl she had once been, who blindly believed the best of everyone. She did not resent her former self for believing a man who had looked her in the eye and sworn he loved her with an undying fervency.

Rather, she wished she could be that lady once more. Oh, how she wished she could look upon perfectly groomed, handsome lords like the earl and the viscount and believe they truly wanted to align themselves with one of the Winters. That their intent was honest, their purpose true.

But she could not.

All it had taken was one letter from Cunningham's former betrothed, the one he *truly* loved, the fine lady he had thrown over because she did not possess the wealth he required, to make her realize how foolish and unreliable her own judgment had been. And then, when she had ended their betrothal before it was public knowledge, Cunningham had waged a ruthless campaign against her. Spreading ghastly lies, courting gossipmongers as if it were his profession.

Leaving her reputation sullied.

She was tarnished, though she had never done anything wrong, aside from believing in Cunningham's lies. She knew it. Everyone she loved knew it.

Her beloved sisters, protected and doted upon by their older brother Dev, were every bit as vulnerable as she had been. Every bit as in danger of being taken advantage of and subsequently ruined by fortune-hunting scoundrels who smiled with their lips and lied with their tongues.

Her sisters were lambs for the slaughter, as it were. With the possible exception of Grace, who did not suffer fools and who saw through everything and everyone. And of course Bea, who Eugie had only just discovered was set to wed their brother's right-hand man, Merrick Hart. Though Eugie was not yet entirely convinced Merrick himself was not a fortune hunter…

But that was another matter.

On a sigh, Eugie turned yet another corner in the holly maze, only to discover she was not alone. There, at the other end of the narrow corridor in which she found herself, was the Earl of Hertford, the man who continued to intrude upon her thoughts.

Only to fret over how unsuitable a match he would prove for her sisters, of course.

He, too, was in the act of walking. Striding toward her, his large, powerful body a symmetry of masculine strength. Muscled thighs clad in breeches which did nothing to hide his form, polished riding boots to his knees, his broad shoulders hugged by a well-cut greatcoat.

Beneath the shadow of the brim of his hat, he was undeniably handsome. Too handsome, really. Why could he not have a lumpy middle, or a missing tooth? Why did he have to make her heart thump faster?

She stopped where she was, boots crunching in the frozen gravel, watching him warily. Though the day was a bright one, clouds overhead produced a small torrent of snow flurries, falling from the sky in a smattering of wisps. It was all rather idyllic, except for the man.

"My lord," she greeted, injecting some of the frost of the air into her voice as she dipped into a curtsy. "What are you doing in the gardens? I believed all the gentlemen otherwise occupied with sport and leisure."

He bowed in return, his expression solemn. "Is not a turn in the gardens both sport and leisure?"

She ought to make a hasty escape, and she knew it. Lady Emilia had been stern with her lectures about observing propriety, especially on Eugie's part. There was to be absolutely no time alone with gentlemen. Certainly not handsome gentlemen who were unexpectedly lingering in gardens, far out of sight of the rest of the house party.

"Perhaps it is," she allowed. "Though I do believe it depends upon one's preferred sport and one's preferred leisure."

The moment she had spoken the words, she wished she could recall them.

Although spoken in innocence, given her reputation, they now hung in the air like sordid invitations. She only realized it too late, and felt her cheeks flush, much to her chagrin.

He said nothing. Simply stared at her for so long she feared she would be the first to break. Until, at last, he saved her. "I enjoy gardens. There is something so peaceful about them. Was it not Cicero who said *if you have a garden in your library, everything will be complete*?"

"He was right." She had always liked gardens. Until they had moved to the home next door to her sister-in-law's, the Winter siblings had never dwelled in a home which had boasted gardens, *true* gardens. "Gardens and libraries are two of my favorite places to be."

A sudden gust of cool wind whipped past her then with such force, it caught her bonnet and lifted it from her head. The smart little piece of millinery—newly acquired with her sister-in-law's approval—sailed through the air and landed at the earl's feet like nothing so much as a felled bird.

Eugie started forward, determined to catch it lest another burst of air send it flying once more. She sank to her knees, reaching for it at the same time as Hertford, and their heads knocked together. The surprise pain sent her to her rump in an undignified heap.

"Are you injured, Miss Winter?" the earl asked solicitously, something in the tenor of his voice changing and deepening.

For the first time, he sounded sincere. She could not shake the impression she was hearing and seeing the real him for the first time. It was as if the polite mask he wore had been momentarily lifted.

His concerned face loomed before her.

"I…" There was his luscious mouth again, taunting her. She forgot what to say for an indeterminate span of time as heat unfurled inside her, chasing away the early winter's chill. "Yes. That is to say, *no*. I am not terribly injured. Forgive me, my lord. I have always had a bad habit of forgetting to tie my bonnets in place."

He stood and held his gloved hand out to her.

She stared at it for a moment before accepting his aid. The earl pulled her to her feet with a fluid ease and grace that left her feeling weightless. And all too aware of how near to each other they suddenly were. She could see the striations of gold, green, and cinnamon in his gaze, the fine shadow of whiskers on his angled jaw.

Even his eyebrows were handsome, perfect slashes above his unique eyes. Strange she had never noticed such a feature on a man before, unless the brows in question were bushy as twin caterpillars.

Something was wrong with her, surely. The knock to her head had addled her wits.

He settled her hat where it belonged with ginger care. "There you are, back in place."

But instead of taking a step in retreat and putting some much-needed distance between them, he lingered. Their eyes held. She forgot to breathe.

Eugie could not have been more startled when his fingers grazed the underside of her chin as he tied the ribbon for her. She inhaled suddenly, the cold air sharp and almost painful in her lungs. A welcome distraction from the unwanted sensations he made her feel.

"Thank you, Lord Hertford," she forced herself to say.

A strange, wicked notion occurred to her, from out of nowhere. It was the perfect solution to the problem which had been plaguing her ever since her brother Dev had gotten this misguided notion into his overprotective mind that all his sisters must marry noblemen.

She could determine for herself which of the suitors present at the house party were worthy of her sisters and which decidedly were not. She could discern the fortune hunters from the gentlemen, the scoundrels and the rakes from the genuine and honest. She could distinguish between those who were truly appreciative of her sisters and the men who simply needed to marry their fortunes. Each potential suitor she investigated and found deficient would be one less fortune hunter her sisters needed to guard their hearts and reputations against.

Since her reputation already hung in tatters, she was the one who must do the deed.

She saw it all clearly now.

Yes, it must be her.

And she would begin here and now, with the Earl of Hertford.

She rose on her toes before she lost her daring and pressed her lips to his.

The contact was startling. His mouth was warm, smooth, and supple. Softer than she had expected. The only other man she had kissed, Baron Cunningham, had been thin-lipped, his mouth wet. Her first reaction to this kiss was that the Earl of Hertford's lips felt as fine as they looked.

Her second reaction was *dear, sweet Lord, I am kissing the Earl of Hertford.*

She inhaled swiftly. A mistake, as it happened, because she breathed in his scent. Shaving soap and man. And she *liked* that scent. Liked it far too much. And that scent initiated a wave of something wicked crashing over her.

In the next moment, everything changed.

Because she was not merely pressing her mouth to his. He was kissing her back. His gloved hands were on her face, holding her as if she were made of gossamer. His lower lip was fitted between hers as if it were where it belonged. Everything about this kiss, this moment, felt right in an instinctive way. Even in the depths of her scarred heart.

She told herself it was because this man, unlike Cunningham, allowed her to retain the power while seductively asserting his own. He kissed her, and yet the moment, the kiss, was hers to break. One step backward, and it would all end. But she did not want it to end.

She wanted it to go on.

And on.

Somehow, her hands found his shoulders. His mouth angled over hers, deepening the kiss. His tongue traced the seam of her lips, begging entrance she could not deny. She opened for him, and then he was licking into her mouth, and the taste of him invaded her much the way his scent had. Deep and dark and mysterious, sweet with a bitter hint of coffee.

This kiss was not like anything she had experienced before.

This kiss, she knew instinctively, would ruin any others that would come after it. This kiss was air, it was sunlight, it was a heartbeat.

Necessary.

He made a low sound in his throat. A soft hum of acquiescence escaped her. She was kissing him back, learning how to mold her lips against his, how to move her tongue, to dip it inside his mouth. Somehow, her hands were no longer on his shoulders, but rather in his hair. The thick strands felt delicious to her fingertips beneath the barrier of her own gloves.

She had never before touched a gentleman's hair, but the Earl of Hertford's glossy light-brown locks were soft and thick. He kissed her harder as she caught the strands in her grasp and tugged. He liked it, she discovered, and she liked it too.

She liked it too much.

She liked *him* too much.

This was meant to be an exercise in aiding her sisters, she reminded herself as her tongue forayed into his mouth. She was kissing him to strike him from the list. Testing him. She did not like him. This kiss meant nothing.

Nothing at all.

"Eugie!"

In the end, it was not the practical concerns of her rational mind which made her end the foolishness to which she had succumbed, but rather the sound of her name echoing through the garden. The sound of her name called in the voice of one of the sisters she intended to protect.

Grace, as it happened.

A sobering reminder, indeed.

Eugie took a step backward, abruptly severing the kiss, although it was the last thing the most sinful part of her truly wished to do. She knew her sister, and if Grace was looking for her, it meant her sister was in trouble of her own.

She pressed her fingers over her tingling lips, staring at the earl who had just radically altered everything she thought she had known about herself. "I must go. I should never have…"

The earl's expression was inscrutable, as always. He was rigid and beautiful and perfect, as if he knew not a care in the world, when all Eugie knew was cares. Bearing a fortune for one's dowry was not as trouble-free as others would like to believe. She was renowned and reviled in equal measures, and half the polite world believed horrid falsehoods about her.

Likely, the earl was among them.

"Forgive me, Miss Winter," he offered suddenly, breaking the hollow quiet of the silence that had descended between them.

"Only if you forgive me, my lord, for my inexcusable lapse in judgment," she forced herself to say.

But her swollen mouth disagreed. And so did the heat boiling through her veins. Everything else said kissing him had been wondrous. Perfect.

"Of course," he told her, sounding horridly stilted for a man who had just kissed her until her knees had turned to pudding. "We shall strike it from our minds, and it will most assuredly never happen again."

"Eugie!" called Grace once more.

"Most assuredly not," she agreed, still lingering in spite of her words, mesmerized by his mouth. His handsome face. That way he had about him, so unlike any man she had met before, which made her feel beautiful and graceful and worthy all at once. And not just because he wanted her fortune, either.

But that was all a fantasy as well, wasn't it? For surely, every gentleman in attendance at this godforsaken house party was looking for a wealthy wife. Namely, herself or one of her sisters.

And thinking of her sisters reminded her she needed to protect them.

And thinking of her sisters made her think—

"Eugenia Flora Winter!" Grace hollered, her voice growing nearer. "You may as well answer me, for I know you are the only one mad enough to go traipsing in a frozen garden."

"Apparently, she is wrong," Eugie blurted to the earl. "There are two of us mad enough to do so. Three, if you count Grace."

"Eugie!" Grace's tone was becoming exasperated.

"Go to your sister, my lady," Lord Hertford urged her, his countenance grim. "It would be most unwise for us to be caught alone together. I should not wish to cause further damage to your reputation."

His choice of words was not lost upon her. *Further damage.* She knew for certain then that he was all too aware of the spurious rumors the baron had been spreading about her to everyone who would listen.

She should have said something to that. Something to defend herself. Something to correct his assumptions about her. Assumptions she had likely just enhanced by her unspeakably forward conduct.

But in the end, she said nothing. It did not matter, after all. She had only kissed him to strike him off the list. She curtseyed and then fled. By the time she nearly collided with her sister, her heart was almost back to its normal, even pace.

Only her burning lips and the memory of the earl's mouth on hers remained.

Chapter Three

THE LIBRARY AT Abingdon House was immense. Two stories, lit with floor-to-ceiling mullioned windows at one end and warmed by the cheerful comfort of a massive stone hearth at the other, it was just the sort of place one hid one's self at a country house party. Especially when the rest of the guests were otherwise occupied and when the gentleman in need of hiding was boiling in a scalding pot of his own shame.

In his distress, Cam had paced the length of the library at least a dozen times. He had scoured the shelves for distraction and found none which could sufficiently serve such a purpose.

Reasoning all the tomes on the first floor were histories, Latin, and religious treatises, he had gone upstairs. The second level held no more diversion than the first had. Now, he was pacing a different carpet with the same set of worries weighing upon him.

Because he had done the unthinkable.

He had kissed the Winter with the worst reputation. The one who had worn the red evening gown. The lively, beautiful one with warm, brown eyes that deepened to molten chocolate after she had been kissed. The one with the full lips and the charming brunette curls that fluttered over her face when the wind blew. The Winter who liked gardens and libraries and who had allowed that despicable blighter

Cunningham untold liberties.

The notion of the baron having touched her first ought to have been enough to send him running in the opposite direction. It should have made his only response to the sudden press of her lips to his in the garden a hasty step in retreat.

Yes, he should have ended it before it had begun. One did not go about kissing unwed ladies in gardens. One did not go about kissing unwed ladies *at all*. Kisses and passions and lust decidedly lived in the realm occupied by a gentleman's mistress.

Not that he had one. He and Cecily had parted ways months ago when he had been unable to afford to keep her in the home and jewels she required. Perhaps that was the problem.

Mayhap going so long without bedding a woman had rendered him incapable of determining right from wrong. For surely, he would never have reacted in such a fashion to a woman like Miss Eugie Winter, who was bold and improper and altogether the opposite of what he wanted in a wife.

He would never have kissed her back if he…

Oh, Christ. He passed a hand over his face. Who was he fooling? Yes, he would have. Even with a hundred Cecilys warming his bed, he would have. He would always kiss Miss Eugie Winter back. Because she was beautiful, and she forgot to tie her bonnet in place, and she was daring. Because she held her head high when every room in which she stood abounded with whispers.

He was still pacing when the library door clicked open and the sound of feminine giggles reached him. He stopped, mid-stride, wondering if there was an assignation about to take place below.

Sweet Lord, please no.

"Do you not think Dev will notice we are missing?" asked

a female voice he recognized all too well. After all, it had only been a scant few hours since he had last heard it.

Eugie.

An indelicate snort followed her question. "He is far too occupied making eyes at Lady Emilia to notice we exist," said her companion, presumably one of her sisters.

Eugie sighed. "Thank heavens. I find myself growing weary of all this nonsense. Why does he not simply have us all stand in the great hall and accept the winning bidder for each of our hands?"

"Do not suggest such a thing to him, I beg you," said her sister, though which Winter sister it was, he could not say. "Tomorrow morning, we shall all be trotting out to the great hall to await our miserable fates, no better than the heads of all the wretched animals hanging from the walls."

That was rather a grim notion of matrimony, he thought, frowning to himself as he edged nearer to the railing lining the upper floor of the library. The floor creaked. Of course, it did. He stopped, holding his breath, hoping he remained sufficiently out of sight from below.

"Did you hear that?" Eugie asked her sister. "It sounded as if there was someone walking above. Do you suppose we are not alone?"

He moved backward, avoiding the loud floorboard and blending with the shadows as he heard the ladies below move about.

"You see?" The sister's voice was triumphant. "There is no one there. Everyone is occupied with charades."

"I did not see Lord Hertford," Eugie said quietly.

It was awful of him to eavesdrop upon such a dialogue, he knew. But now that his name had been mentioned, he could not very well descend to the floor below and make himself known. A gentleman would have done so before now.

Apparently, he was not a gentleman. Not where Eugie Winter was concerned.

"Speaking of the arrogant earl," said the sister, "you never did tell me what you thought of him after the dance you shared at the ball."

"I thought nothing of him," Eugie replied, her tone light. "He is a fortune hunter like all the rest, of course."

Eugie's words nettled him.

Because they were true.

But also, because he had no choice in the matter. He had never wanted his dissolute sire to deplete the familial coffers until there was almost nothing left. Until he was forced to count tallows and beg creditors for additional time. Until he had been forced to prepare the selling off of estates that were not a part of the entail just to keep food upon the table.

And because she had kissed him. Surely their kisses had meant something to her…

"Nothing at all?" her sister was saying. "I did think you were watching him with a queer expression on your face afterward."

"You and your observations," Eugie said dismissively. "I know you fancy yourself incredibly skilled at reading faces, but I hate to tell you that you are wrong. Wildly so."

"Come now," said her sister. "Do you not think him handsome, in a suitably arrogant fashion?"

Arrogant? It occurred to him that this was the Winter sister's second use of the word to describe him in less than the same number of minutes. His jaw clenched. What a bit of baggage she was. He hoped it was not the sister Aylesford intended to make his pretend bride. The dowager would never accept such a cynical creature for her beloved grandson.

"I suppose he is, if one likes brown hair," Eugie said, her tone nonchalant.

She *supposed* he was handsome? If one liked brown hair? The minx had brown hair herself. Who was she to cast judgment?

"His hair is rather too light for me," said her sister. "I prefer black hair myself."

"That is because your heart is black," quipped Eugie.

And on this matter, for a change, he could not disagree.

"I am pragmatic," argued the sister. "There is a difference."

"Oh, and now you shall next tell me your pragmatism is the reason for considering the notion of a feigned betrothal with a rakehell like Viscount Aylesford." Eugie scoffed her disapproval.

Dear Lord. Aylesford had attempted to put his plan into motion. Which meant the Winter sister mystery had likely been solved. It was Miss Grace Winter below, chatting with Eugie.

Unless Aylesford had changed his mind since this morning. And, well, when it came to scoundrels like Aylesford, one could never be sure.

"Think of the beauty of it," Grace Winter was saying below. "All I have to do is agree to a betrothal. Though I am enjoying making Aylesford squirm about what I will decide, it seems a flawless plan. Dev will be overjoyed at the prospect of me becoming Viscountess Aylesford and the future Duchess of... Oh, I do not recall. There are so many of them, you know. The titles all blend."

"Like a patch of weeds in an otherwise sound garden," Eugie added.

What the bloody hell? Impertinent minxes! Did they not realize *they* were the weeds in the garden, and not the other way around? How dare they?

"Precisely," agreed Miss Grace Winter. "But the loveliest

thing of all is that I can have my freedom. By the time I end the betrothal with Aylesford, Bea will be wed, and I expect you, Christabella, and Pru shall be well on your way. I will be free to pursue my own destiny. Lord knows I have no wish to marry anyone, least of all a witless aristocrat whose greatest concern is the knot of his cravat and how much coin he can divert to his mistress."

"No one will wed me on account of the odious Baron Cunningham," Eugie countered.

Just the utterance of the bastard's name was enough to set Cam on edge.

"Oh, pish," dismissed her sister. "You are lovely and smart and kind and funny. Any man who is concerned about the drivel that fool spews is not worthy of you."

Strange, but he was inclined to agree with Miss Grace Winter on this matter, if not any other.

"I wish everyone thought the way you do, Grace, but they do not." Eugie's voice held an undeniable note of sadness. "More than anything, I want to make certain none of the rest of you suffer as I have. It is why I have embarked upon a plan."

He did not like the sadness in her voice. It did not suit her. Happiness and laughter and smiles suited a woman like Miss Eugie Winter. But he could not say anything now. Not when he had been silent for so long, lingering and overhearing her private dialogue with her sister.

"A plan?" Grace rubbed her hands together, the sound unmistakable. "Do tell. I adore plans, as you well know."

"Yes." Eugie hesitated before continuing. "I am working my way through all the eligible gentlemen in attendance and kissing them. I began with Lord Hertford, if you must know."

A low sound of denial left him before he could contain it. Surely she had not kissed him as part of some ludicrous plan to protect her sisters, had she? Surely the kiss had been real. The things he had felt, the spark between them, the way her lips had moved in response, the way her tongue had writhed against his, had not been all part of some bloodless, passionless plan.

Had it?

"Did you hear that?" Grace queried below, her voice curious.

"Hear what?" Eugie asked.

"That noise," elaborated her sister. "It sounded like a wounded animal."

Good Christ. He leaned his head against the wall of books behind him and closed his eyes, sure his ignominy could not grow any worse.

"Probably the wind outside," Eugie dismissed. "It has been howling since this morning. I nearly lost my bonnet."

He recalled, all too well, retrieving her bonnet for her, their heads bumping, fingers brushing, their stares melding. The kisses that had come afterward. Part of her *plan*, it would appear. It required every speck of control he possessed to remain where he was instead of stomping down the spiral staircase and making his presence known.

No good could come of this, he was sure.

"You never did remember to tie your ribbons," her sister was saying below. "But tell me about this plan of yours. Kissing all the eligible gentlemen, you say?"

"Yes," Eugie agreed. "I will happily spare you the misery of a marriage predicated upon nothing more than your fortunes. A man cannot woo one sister and then move on to another, after all, and if he does, woe to him, for he has not yet met the Winter sisters."

"A sound plan," Miss Grace Winter offered grudgingly. "Except it sounds rather taxing. Only think of how many gentlemen are in attendance. Do you truly mean to kiss them all?"

"If I must. I would do anything to save you from the suffering I have endured at the hands of the baron," Eugie said.

"A dreadful little toad of a man he is," agreed Grace. "But forget that rotter. I am chiefly concerned with you. How do you propose to go about kissing so many gentlemen? Your lips will grow chapped and withered."

The thought of Miss Eugie Winter kissing all the gentlemen in attendance made him want to do violence. The notion of her soft, supple lips going dry with the effort had him clenching his fists. He told himself he ought not to be affected by her. After all, she had just admitted to her sister that kissing him had been a part of her scheme to save her sisters from heartache.

Noble, he supposed.

But foolish, also.

And he could not deny the blow his pride received upon the revelation.

He thought she had kissed him because she wanted to, because she had been moved by the same odd connection between them he had felt. Altogether unwanted, and yet equally undeniable.

He could still feel her kiss upon his lips. Her taste was yet upon his tongue. Tentative and deliciously sweet, like a ripe berry plucked in the heart of summer. She had kissed him as if she would never kiss another again. As if kissing him was all she required, more than her next breath.

And the way her fingers had settled into his hair, grabbing tufts and pulling with such exquisite, painful pleasure…

"Do you not think the idea a sound one?" Eugie asked her sister below, cutting into his wild thoughts.

Tell her, he urged Miss Grace Winter in his mind. *Make certain she abandons this ludicrous plan altogether.*

"It is brilliant, I agree," Grace said, shattering his hopes she would have enough common sense to overrule her sister and make her see the error of her ways. "I wish I had thought of it myself, in fact. But to be perfectly candid, I would far prefer a false engagement with a scoundrel like Lord Aylesford than having to kiss my way through all these spoiled lords."

"I do not blame you," Eugie told her sister. "Finding what you need in a feigned engagement ought to suit your purpose perfectly. Because I am the only one among us with a tarnished reputation I am the one who must do it."

"You began with the Earl of Hertford, you say," Grace ventured, her tone curious now. "How was it? The kiss, I mean. Aylesford did not make an effort to try just yet. For a supposed rake, he has an appalling lack of motivation."

"Oh, it…" Eugie paused, and Cam held his breath as she sought words.

Defied explanation.

Changed everything.

Shook me to my core.

Any of those would have been acceptable responses.

Instead, Miss Eugenia Winter said, "It was passable, I suppose."

And the battle lines were most distinctly drawn.

Chapter Four

$\mathcal{T}$HE AFTERNOON FOLLOWING the kisses she had shared with the Earl of Hertford, Eugie had decided upon her next target. She had forced herself to realize Lord Hertford was an unrepentant fortune hunter, regardless of the way his kisses had seemed to alter her world, just the same as all the other gentlemen in attendance, men who were either desperate for a bride or a fortune.

For some of them, it was both.

Either way, her devotion to her sisters was complete. She would do what she must to make certain none of them would find themselves being taken advantage of by a scoundrel who thought nothing of their true hearts.

Her brother Dev was fair and just, but they had all tried disabusing him of the notion they must wed, and he had remained convinced he had gathered the best of the best for this house party, all the better to find them husbands.

Sometimes, Eugie knew, her brother could not see how wrong he was. Sometimes, arguing with the stubborn but beloved man was not worth the effort. And so, she would step into the protective role in a way he could not.

Lord Ashley Rawdon had been eying her sister Pru as if she were a dessert course and he could not decide if he wanted to consume her in small bites or eat her all at once. Dreadful fellow, with a reputation that preceded him as one of the worst scoundrels in all London. Indeed, her brother Dev would have never sanctioned his invitation were it not for his brother, the Duke of Coventry, who was also in attendance.

The handsome duke was awkward and quiet.

His equally gorgeous brother did all the talking for him.

"And now for a game of charades," Lady Emilia announced to the assemblage, who had gathered in the drawing room, awaiting the next round of entertainments she had prepared for them.

Her sister-in-law was doing a tremendous job of amusing the guests assembled. Indeed, Eugie could not find fault with the parlor games she had arranged. It was to her credit that such a massive assembly could be easily shepherded from one diversion to the next.

But charades was one of Eugie's least favorite games. So much guessing. So many people who were lackluster at mimicry. So much time wasted. Fortunately for her, Lord Ashley appeared to be making his way to the doorway of the drawing room, all the better to secure his exit.

He had the right idea, even if she did not trust him one whit when it came to Pru. Or any of her other sisters, for that matter. Slowly, Eugie worked her way through the crowd, maneuvering herself to the door. She had been making a habit of escape recently. And it never failed to surprise her just how easy it was.

Casting her gaze about to make certain no one was watching her, she slipped through the door. Charades could go to the devil for all she cared. What did concern her was her sisters and their hearts. Lord Ashley was a scoundrel of the first order, she was certain of it. All she had to do was find him…

Down the hall she went, but Lord Ashley's legs were longer than hers. And he was quicker. He was disappearing around the bend in the hall by the time she was following him.

"Miss Winter."

A voice stopped her.

A familiar voice.

Warmth unfurled, settling in her core. She spun about, and there he stood. The Earl of Hertford.

She could do nothing more than stare at him, wondering what he wanted. Why he was so handsome. Why she could not kiss him again.

But then she realized she was standing about like a ninny, gawking at him in silence. How odd she must appear. How awkward. Once more, they were beyond the bounds of propriety, standing alone in the hall. The drawing room was not far from them, filled with revelers. At any moment, one of them could exit the chamber, walk into the hall, and find the two of them alone.

She should go.

Follow Lord Ashley. Make certain he was not the heartless fortune hunter she suspected he was. Kiss him.

But the thought of kissing the rakish Lord Ashley, in spite of his undeniable good looks, only left her feeling hollow and cold inside. Perhaps she could attempt to kiss him another day, she told herself. There was no reason to begin her plan today.

"My lord," she said to the earl. "Forgive me, but I have a headache. I was about to seek my chamber and have a restoring nap."

"Oh?" He eyed her, his gaze raking her form in a fashion that was far more familiar than it had been before.

She liked it.

"Yes, I was," she said stupidly.

Because he was looking at her with such intensity she

could scarcely form a coherent word. Fire burned to life within her. And there was his mouth, that perfectly formed masterpiece she had not been able to stop thinking about after she had last felt it moving against hers.

She had told Grace the kiss had been passable. *What rot.* Nothing she had ever experienced in her life deserved to be described in such an unenthusiastic fashion less.

"Allow me to escort you, my lady," he offered, sounding perfectly polite.

An utter gentleman.

But no gentleman escorted a lady to her chamber. She may be a wicked Winter, but she knew the rules. She knew propriety. Lady Emilia had made certain of it.

She ought to deny him. Tell him she was fine. To leave her alone.

She opened her mouth. "Very well," said her traitorous tongue. "To the west wing, if you please. That shall be far enough."

It was a tradeoff, of sorts, she supposed. A nod to propriety, however small.

And then her equally traitorous hand settled upon the crook of his elbow, and off they went, into the intricate web of Abingdon House halls.

CAM WAS BEHAVING very much out of character for himself, and he knew it. But he had not been able to excise the taunting, dulcet voice of Miss Eugie Winter from his mind after inadvertently playing the eavesdropper the day before.

It was passable, I suppose.

Passable?

She *supposed?*

The words still nettled. It was those words, he told himself, and surely not the desire to feel her lips beneath his once more, that had set him upon the ruinous path down which he now marched. Her hand upon his arm was as light as a butterfly, and yet he felt it through the layers of his coat and shirt like a brand.

Her scent invaded his senses like a charging cavalry brigade. *Christ*, she smelled like a hothouse in verdant bloom. Floral, rich, and exotic.

Desire, unwanted and fierce, surged through him. His breeches were suddenly too tight as he strode at her side, and he could honestly say he had never in all his thirty years gotten a cockstand whilst promenading with a lady.

Until today.

But Eugie Winter was no lady, as her reputation proved. Nothing had made that more apparent than her forward behavior yesterday in the garden, when she had all but flung herself into his arms and kissed him. To say nothing of the plan she had revealed to her sister in the library. Kissing every gentleman in attendance, indeed.

The reminder filled him with a rush of possessiveness so strong and unexpected, he directed them through the nearest door. As it happened, the chamber was thankfully unoccupied. A cursory glance suggested it was a writing room.

"Lord Hertford," she protested, "what are you doing? I thought you were escorting me to the west wing."

He closed the door at their backs and took her in his arms. Never mind her arms slid around his neck as if that were where they belonged. He did his best to ignore the delicious swell of her breasts crushing into his chest. Her eyes widened. The lashes were long and thick.

He thought of her in another man's arms like this. In that scoundrel Lord Ashley's arms, whom she had been following when he had interrupted her and her ludicrous plan both. And then he remembered his own plan, the one he had formed in the darkness of his chamber last night whilst he had been plagued by thoughts of her lush lips.

He was going to give her the best damned kiss of her life.

A kiss to make her swoon.

A kiss she would never forget.

"I have heard," he told her, his voice low, "the best cure for a headache is a kiss. Mayhap we ought to try it. I should hate to see you suffer, my dear Miss Winter."

Her nose wrinkled, the most adorable expression of befuddlement crossing her features. "You have?"

He nodded. "Of course. It is not common knowledge, you know. But I thought perhaps to give it an attempt."

"Oh." She blinked, then the pink tip of her tongue flicked slowly over her ripe bottom lip. "Yes, that would be agreeable. How solicitous of you to offer your aid, my lord."

Anchoring her to him with one hand at her waist, he drew the other to her face. His thumb passed over her lip. Just once. He was not supposed to be enjoying this. He was supposed to be teaching her a lesson.

Instead, he was teaching himself one.

In desire.

Because now that he had Eugie Winter in his grasp, her head tipped back, her lips his for the taking, need slammed into him, full force. It took his breath. It took his will. And he could do nothing but stand there, astounded.

She was everything he should not want. Being here with her, alone, touching her, about to kiss her once more, was wrong. If they were caught, he would have to wed her. He had lived his life without the tiniest blot of scandal to his name. He was the Prince of Proper. He had never sought an unmarried lady in such a bold manner. He had never wanted to.

What was it about this dark-haired, dark-eyed merchant's daughter that made him so bloody weak?

"Are you going to do it?" she whispered, her gaze dipping to his mouth.

"Yes," he said thickly, barely managing the word past another raging wave of pure, unadulterated lust. "I was giving you the chance to acquaint yourself to the notion."

He had never wanted another woman in the way he wanted her. It was visceral and real, pumping through his veins, warming his blood, hardening his cock even more. It was elemental, the sort of raw desire he had only ever allowed himself to entertain toward ladies of the demimonde. But it was more than that. So much more.

"Lord Hertford," she said, sounding breathless.

He lowered his head a fraction, unable to resist inhaling her addictive scent once more. "Yes?"

"I am acquainted," she said. "You may kiss me now."

Damnation. He was meant to be the one wooing her, and yet she was doing all the wooing. For the first time in his life, he wished he had been a devoted rakehell. But then he forgot to think. Because Miss Eugie Winter rose to her tiptoes and pressed her mouth to his once more.

It was the only spur he required.

The spell she cast over him broke, along with the reins of his control. His fingers plunged into the upsweep of her hair, the place where all her curls were tidily kept trapped. He wanted them free and wild.

His mouth crushed hers. On a groan of pure desire, he swept his tongue over the seam of her lips, and when she opened, he surged inside. She tasted of the sweet desserts of luncheon. Berry custard and cream and something else he could not define.

Something that was specifically, deliciously, Eugie Winter.

Full stop.

Hair pins were raining to the floor in a hail of dull little thumps. He hated the gloves he wore, for the way they inhibited him from feeling the texture of her hair. Spun silk, he was sure. The hand on her waist traveled to her back, coasting up her spine, pressing her closer to him as he ravished her mouth.

Her tongue toyed with his, unabashed. It was the most carnal kiss he had ever shared. Not even his mistresses had kissed him with such wild abandon. No, indeed, theirs had been precise, measured. They had known how to control the pace with the pressure of their lips, the soft, subtle response of their desires.

But not the woman in his arms.

She kissed him as if she wanted to consume him.

And, *Lord God*, he wanted her to do just that. He could not think of another thought but her. She was all he wanted, all he tasted, all he felt, all he desired. His plan dissipated. Nothing else mattered but the need to claim her, to make her his.

Kissing her still, he moved them as one. Across the floor. He had spied a settee upon their initial entrance, and he instinctively aimed for it now, backing her up, leading the way one step at a time as he plundered her lips. How sweet her response was. How intoxicating her curves, pressed against him.

He thought it was possible she was the most desirable woman he had ever met. Not because of her beauty, but because of the fiery passion within her. The way her body seemed to be made for his. He had never before felt such a connection with a woman as he did with her. He felt it to the marrow of his bones, to the heart of him. There was only one word for it...*right*.

Perfectly right, even when it was all wrong.

Even when everything about it was wicked. Improper. Even when he was going further than he had intended. He broke their kiss when they reached the settee, gratified to find her cheeks flushed, her brown eyes dark and glazed, her full lips delectably swollen from his kisses.

"How is your headache?" he felt compelled to ask for the sake of politeness, leaning his forehead into hers.

"It is...fine," she said on a sigh.

"I lied about kisses curing headaches," he admitted before kissing her again. Just one more drugging sip from her lips. She was like an elixir, and he could not get enough.

He withdrew at last, breathless and aching for her.

"I lied about having a headache," she whispered, her gaze unwavering, burning into his.

"We are both of us liars, it would seem," he said softly. "Sinners."

"Yes," she agreed, tipping up her chin and rubbing her lower lip along his in the most erotic half kiss he had experienced.

In the *only* half kiss he had ever experienced. When had half kisses become something one did? He did not know. None of his mistresses had ever done so, he was sure of it. All he *did* know was that it made him more desperate for her than before.

Bloody hell.

He had to slow down. In truth, he had to leave this chamber.

But he could not. He could not leave her side. And not just because of his plan. Not just because he wanted to thwart her. But because of *her*.

Because she was mouthwatering and breath-stealing, and she was fire to his ice, and he wanted to melt.

"We should go," he told her anyway, the small part of his mind still capable of reasoning chiming in. "I should escort you to the west wing as I promised. As a gentleman would do."

"What if I do not wish for you to be a gentleman?" she asked.

Fuck.

One question from her, and his cock was more rigid than ever, straining at the falls of his breeches.

"Sit," he rasped.

It was the only word he could manage.

She stared at him for a beat, looking as if she wanted to challenge him. Indeed, part of him expected her to. But in the end, she settled upon the settee. And not with a bit of grace. Here was evidence she was not as practiced in the art of seduction as her kisses would suggest. She had dropped to the cushion with such force, the gilded wooden frame slid into the wall with a loud thump.

Some distant part of his mind wondered if anyone would overhear and come to investigate. But the rest of him only saw Miss Eugie Winter in a diaphanous billow of seafoam-colored skirts. Her dark curls were coming undone, trailing over her shoulders. Her red lips were parted. She was the most alluring sight he had ever beheld, even set against the backdrop of dark-green walls and hunting pictures.

And there was only one thing he could do.

He sank to his knees before her.

Chapter Five

*T*HE EARL OF Hertford was on his knees before her.

Surely, nothing good could come of this.

She was old enough to know better. World-weary enough—thanks to the odious Baron Cunningham—to understand just how great a risk she took. One kiss was all she had given the baron, and he had turned that anthill into a mountain of pain and shame. Allowing liberties to any man, let alone another fortune-hunting peer, was the last thing she ought to be doing.

She had her plan to see through, she reminded herself.

Or, at least, she *tried* to remind herself. Thinking anything at all was becoming dreadfully difficult. Especially with a man as beautiful as the earl staring at her. And especially when he slid his hands beneath the hem of her gown.

Definitely when he settled his hands upon her ankles and caressed a path upward, over her calves.

Eugie stared at him, hunger coursing through her, a throbbing ache pulsing from between her thighs and drawing outward, overtaking everything. Their gazes were locked upon each other. She had never in her life been more painfully aware of the unwanted barrier of a gentleman's gloves and her own silk stockings.

How she wanted his bare skin on hers.

Even if this was wrong.

And it was wrong, she reminded herself as his wicked hands traveled to her knees, caressing the sensitive dips behind them.

Very wrong indeed, she scolded herself as he gently guided her legs apart.

Horridly wrong. But he had lifted the hems of her gown and petticoat so they rested in her lap in a soft heap, and still, she could not muster one word of denial. Because she did not want to deny him.

He was stiff and proper, gentlemanly and aloof. And yet, when he came to life, he was an inferno. And she wanted to get burned.

"Miss Winter," he said.

His voice was a caress. Low and liquid.

"Call me Eugie," she implored, because she could not bear for such formality between them when he was seeing her limbs encased in stockings and garters.

"Eugie," he repeated, as if trying it out on his tongue.

She liked it. Liked the way it sounded. Liked the intimacy it gave them. Liked everything about this forbidden moment and this equally forbidden man far, far too much.

But then, his hands were moving higher, over her thighs, and she forgot to think entirely. Words were elusive. All she could do was feel. His head dipped. And his mouth, his beautiful mouth, laid a kiss upon her inner thigh. Who would have imagined a kiss upon such a place? Or how glorious it felt?

A soft moan escaped her as hunger built. Tension drawing into a knot in her core.

But in the next moment, all that dissipated when the door to the chamber opened and her sister stepped over the threshold. Lord Hertford was quick in his reaction, but not quick enough that Grace would have no doubt something untoward had been occurring.

"Eugie, what in heaven's name are you about?" Grace asked, her tone scandalized.

The earl had flipped down her skirts, but now he stood, offering an abbreviated bow to Grace. "Miss Winter. I am afraid the other Miss Winter was suffering from a h—"

"Splinter," Eugie interrupted before he gave further legs to her initial prevarication. Grace was intelligent. She would not be swayed by the suggestion Lord Hertford had been attempting to ease her headache by rucking up her skirts. "I had a splinter in my heel. A heel splinter."

Grace's eyes narrowed. She looked distinctly unimpressed. "You had a splinter."

Eugie swallowed. "Yes."

"She did," added the earl, his expression guilty as sin.

The man was terrible at subterfuge, wasn't he?

"In your heel," Grace continued.

"Yes," Eugie said weakly, knowing her hasty attempt at deception would not prove sufficient either. She could only hope Grace would hold her tongue and would not question—

"Was there a need to raise your hem past your knees?" her fiendish sister asked.

Eugie scowled at her. "Yes. As it happens, they kept falling over my foot. I could not see my heel properly, and Lord Hertford was kind enough to offer his assistance. I am most indebted to him."

"How...*kind* of his lordship to offer such attentive *aid*," Grace said, smirking.

Eugie imagined all the ways in which she would get even with her sister later.

For now, she stood, swishing her skirts back into place. Her heart was still pounding steadily. Her body was still aching. And the longing he had incited within her had yet to be doused. If anything, she was all the more desperate to know what she had missed.

If only Grace had not interrupted them when she had.

But then again, perhaps it was for the best. Perhaps if she had not, Eugie would be compromised in truth now, rather than just compromised in theory. One could not be compromised, after all, when one's ignominy had only been witnessed by one's sister.

Could one?

She forced herself to speak. "It was indeed most kind of the earl, and now, thanks to him, my splinter is removed." She smiled at her sister before casting a frantic glance toward the earl. "You may go now, my lord. It would not do for anyone else to find you here. Thankfully, my sister can be trusted to keep your assistance to me in such a sensitive matter between the three of us. Can you not, Grace dearest?"

She had never before asked her sister to keep a secret from their brother for her, but Eugie would ask it now. She had no wish for Dev to force her to marry the earl, or for him to challenge Hertford to a duel.

Grace hesitated, her eyes narrowing farther, before she responded. "Yes, of course. I will keep your *assistance* with my sister's splinter to myself, particularly since the splinter has been removed and such a scene will not be repeated. Will it?"

The wickedness within Eugie certainly hoped it would.

"Misses Winter," the earl said stiffly, before he bowed to the both of them. "If you ladies will excuse me, I should leave before I cause any undue harm to either of your reputations."

"Yes, do go," Grace said rather rudely.

"Of course," Eugie murmured, glaring at her sister before turning her gaze back to Hertford. "Thank you, my lord."

For kissing me senseless, she wanted to add. Wisely, she refrained. The look he gave her was as scorching as it was brief. And then, he was gone.

Leaving Eugie alone to face her sister.

"What was the Earl of Hertford truly doing beneath your skirts?" Grace demanded when the door had scarcely closed on his lordship's back.

"Lower your voice if you please," Eugie ordered her sister. "I have no wish for such a question to carry."

"Then you should not have been alone with the earl in this room with his hands up your skirts," her sister countered, her tone laden with censure.

Grace was not wrong.

Eugie had no excuse for her actions, save the way being in Lord Hertford's presence made her feel. Perhaps it was his mouth. Or his kisses? Those hazel eyes. The strong, well-defined slash of his jaw. That light-brown hair of his, almost the shade of honey…

"I acted imprudently," she forced herself to say, lest her mind get carried away. The ramifications of her actions descended upon her, filling her cheeks with heat and her heart with regret. "I could have caused great harm to all your reputations, and for that I am sorry. You will not tell Dev, will you?"

Her sister's lips compressed and she gave her a searching look before answering. "Before I make any promises, please tell me the splinter in question was not Lord Hertford's manly appendage."

"Manly appendage?" Eugie's cheeks went hotter still. "Grace!"

"Oh, do not act scandalized with me." Grace took a step closer, her thorough gaze traveling over the mangled remnants of Eugie's coiffure. "You were just allowing a man liberties. Your hair is almost completely unbound, you know. If anyone else were to have come upon you… Never mind. I am getting distracted. You did not answer my question about the dubious splinter."

Of course, she knew to what her sister was referring. Christabella had recently been able to acquire some rather lurid books with the aid of an enterprising lady's maid. Their sister-in-law, Lady Emilia, had also given them a stern talk. But still. His manly appendage?

She could not bear say it aloud.

"There was no splinter," she admitted instead, "as you well know. I was following Lord Ashley, and Lord Hertford approached me out of nowhere. I could not very well admit I was following Lord Ashley so that I could kiss him and remove him from the list."

"You are truly going through with your madcap *kiss all the gentlemen* plan?" Grace demanded. "You do realize how many gentlemen are in attendance and how short the weeks are until Christmas, do you not?"

"I am not intending to kiss *all* the gentlemen," she defended herself. "Just the ones who appear to be courting our sisters and who have suspect motives. Lord Ashley, for instance, is a notorious reprobate. He does not deserve Pru."

"I rather thought he was attempting to arrange a match between Pru and his brother," Grace said then, frowning.

"The duke and Pru?" It was Eugie's turn to frown as she contemplated that. "I do think you must be wrong. Coventry has scarcely spoken a word to Pru."

"He has scarcely spoken a word to anyone," Grace countered. "Indeed, there is something odd about him. He almost never goes about in society, but he is somehow a familiar of Lady Emilia's, which is the only reason he would deign to attend."

"Perhaps I shall not have to kiss Lord Ashley after all," she mused.

"At last we return to you and your scandalous behavior," Grace said. "You were on your way to kiss Lord Ashley, when Lord Hertford waylaid you and you wound up kissing him and allowing him to toss up your skirts instead."

She winced. "When you say it thus, it sounds hideous."

"Because it *is* hideous." Grace's tone was sharp—she had never been one to mince words or spare feelings. "If I did not know you as I do, I would suspect you guilty of all the abominable things that pompous bag of wind accused."

"You know just as well as I that I only ever kissed Lord Cunningham once," she felt compelled to defend, hating how one man's prevarication could follow her for so long. Could ruin her in the eyes of others for a lifetime.

How quick society was to believe a lie as long as it whetted their collective appetite for a good scandal.

"Of course I know that, dearest," Grace reassured her, patting her arm in a rare show of consolation. "But perhaps Lord Hertford does not."

Though her sister's tone was gentle, the implication was clear.

All the warmth burning through her went cold. "You mean to suggest the earl believes the scurrilous rumors Cunningham spread about me?"

Grace's countenance softened with undeniable sympathy. "He has kissed you twice in two days. He has also managed to get you into this room so he could ravish you. Perhaps you ought not to be worried about our sisters, Eugie. Mayhap you should be concerned for yourself."

Dear Lord. Why had she not seen it for herself? Why had she not realized sooner? *I should not wish to cause further damage to your reputation*, he had said in the garden. Which meant not only did the Earl of Hertford know about the gossip surrounding her, he was only kissing her because he believed she would allow him liberties.

He thought she was a trollop.

And she had certainly behaved as one.

"Oh, Grace," she whispered, dread settling over her shoulders like a mantle. "What shall I do?"

"If I were you, I would punch him in the eye," Grace drawled. "But you are too softhearted for violence."

"I think I shall settle for a sound harangue instead."

"Wise choice." Her sister gave her a quelling look. "But no more splinters, real or imagined, or I will be forced to tell Dev after all."

"No more kisses with the earl," she promised Grace.

Why did the thought fill her with disappointment?

WHAT HAD HE been thinking?

Cam stalked from the writing room, castigating himself with each step that took him farther away from his folly. He needed to find a brandy. Or claret. Or anything.

No, he did not. He needed a head-clearing walk in the frigid December air.

He made his way toward the gardens, surprised when Aylesford ambled into view around a bend in the hall, looking as if he had just woken up although it was the midst of the afternoon. Now that he thought upon it, he had not seen his friend at breakfast this morning.

"Aylesford," he greeted him grimly, offering nothing more than a curt smile that was more grimace.

He had every intention of continuing on, moving past the dissolute viscount so he could make sense of his own stupidity.

But Aylesford was otherwise inclined. "Just the man I was looking for this morning."

"It is well past noon," he offered acidly, "and I am not in the mood for a dialogue at the moment."

"Damn me, I slept longer than I had supposed," Aylesford grumbled, passing a hand along his jaw, which was neatly shaven. "Why did Carruthers not tell me it was afternoon? You have not seen my sister or my mother, have you?"

"I have not seen Her Grace or Lady Lydia," he said, thinking the duchess would not be impressed by the viscount's bleary-eyed state. "You had a late night, I take it? One of the matrons or bored wives present warmed your bed all evening, I gather."

"Yes." Aylesford coughed, the blades of his cheekbones darkening. "Something rather like that."

Despite his own state of distraction, Cam noted the lack of sincerity in his friend's tone. Along with the way he suddenly averted his gaze. "Never say it was your feigned betrothed who kept you awake."

Miss Grace Winter seemed a cool sort from his few inter-actions with her and the dialogue he had overheard in the library, but perhaps there was another side to her. Leave it to a rakehell like Aylesford to draw it forth.

The color in the viscount's cheeks deepened. "Lower your tone, man, lest someone hear you. No one knows she is my betrothed just yet."

Cam could not contain his chortle. "We are speaking of the same Miss Grace Winter, are we not? Do you mean to tell me you spent the evening with her?"

His horror was complete. What manner of females were these Winter sisters? They were veritable Sirens, luring otherwise sane men into the rocks with their mere song.

"Damnation, Cam." Casting his gaze wildly about, Ayles-ford gripped his arm and began propelling the both of them toward the doors leading to the frozen outdoor gardens. "If we must speak of such delicate matters, let us do it where no one else shall overhear. There are ears in the walls of every country house. Mark my words."

He could not argue. Just yesterday, he had been the bloody ears Aylesford spoke of. Grimly, he followed his friend into the bleary, cold December day. Overhead, a fine drizzle had begun to unleash from the clouds, lending the air a damp chill he felt to his bones. The heavy door closed with a barely audible creak.

A flock of starlings, unconcerned with the impending winter gloom, took exception to the sound and burst into flight, winging overhead. The gravel crunched beneath their soles as he and Aylesford made their way down a path in silence, their breath puffing clouds into the chill air.

The viscount stopped at last, raking a hand through his dark, wavy locks. "I fell asleep in the library last night," he admitted.

Cam's eyebrows rose. "With Miss Winter?"

"Of course not." His friend scowled. "She made off well before I found my way into her brother's brandy stores."

He could not make one whit of sense from his friend's revelations. "Here, now. Best begin at the beginning, Aylesford. Before the tippling. And the tupping."

His friend's jaw went rigid. "There was no tupping, blast you. Grace is my betrothed. My *feigned* betrothed. Either way, I would not tup her. Listen to you, the Prince of Proper, suggesting I would *tup* the woman I am going to wed."

"Grace?" he could not help but to repeat Aylesford's use of Miss Winter's given name, prodding his friend, who already seemed as if he were harboring conflicting feelings about the feigned betrothed in question. And truly, he could not resist. It was the distraction he needed from his own stupidity. "It certainly sounds as if the two of you are quite intimate."

"Devil take it, Hertford." Despite the sleepiness he had thus far failed to scrub from his eyes, Aylesford appeared genuinely enraged. "I was not intimate with her. I would not dishonor her… Fair enough, I *would* dishonor her, but I am doing my best not to, in an effort to preserve the lady's reputation."

Cam was not fooled one bit. Miss Grace Winter was tougher than a blacksmith's anvil. "She rejected you, did she not?"

"Fuck." Aylesford's scowl turned into a glare. "Yes, she did, if you must know. Let us all revel in the humiliation the great rake Lord Aylesford suffered at the hands of a stubborn, arrogant female whose brother is a glorified factory owner, for God's sake."

He could not contain his laughter, but in truth, it was not at his friend's expense. Rather, he was laughing at the both of them. What a pair they made: the seasoned rakehell and the proper lord, both with their well-earned Town bronze and their knowledge of the finer sex, laid low by the Misses Winter.

"I ought to hit you for laughing at me," the viscount said ruefully, rubbing his jaw once more. "I shan't, because I like you far too much, Hertford. And because the dowager would have my hide if word of it ever reached her."

He caught his breath, wiping tears of mirth from the corners of his eyes. "If it makes you feel any better, I am not laughing at you. I am laughing at the both of us. These Winter sisters are running us ragged."

"Oh?" Aylesford grinned crookedly. "And which sister is running you ragged, may I ask? Could it be the chit in the red dress? Do not try to deny it, Hertford. I knew it from the moment you attempted to dissuade me from pursuing her by bringing up that hogwash story of Cunningham's. You wanted her for yourself. You need not have gone to such an effort to keep me at a distance. If you had but said the words."

The chit in the red dress.

Yes, of course it was Eugie. It had always been Eugie, from the moment he had stepped foot inside Abingdon House and seen her from across the massive hall. He had been drawn to her from the first, although she was *the* Winter with the reputation. There was something ridiculously alluring about her.

"Miss Eugie is…" He paused, struggling to find words apt enough to describe the way she made him feel and finding none. "Yes, she is running me rather ragged."

There were a great many more things he could have said.

Such as *I almost ravished her in the writing room just now.*

Or, *I had her skirts about her waist when your feigned betrothed entered the chamber.*

But why bother?

He was having far too much enjoyment at Aylesford's expense.

"You like her," Aylesford observed, his tone as serious as his gaze. Almost as if he required a validation that the feelings assailing him, too, were real.

"I do," Cam admitted grudgingly. "But she is all wrong for me. I could never make a match with a woman such as her."

Indeed, he had built his reputation upon his strict adherence to propriety. He was always above reproach. Though his friends were rakehells and ne'er-do-wells, he had never made a rustle. Mostly for his mother's sake, he realized now. She had already endured so much for him, and her constitution could not bear much upset.

"Best to keep her at a distance, then," Aylesford said, and Cam knew he was not just speaking of he and Eugie, but of himself and Grace as well.

"Best, yes," he agreed.

"But when has what is best ever been what is most pleasing?" his friend asked, his voice contemplative.

"Never," he agreed.

Still, he knew, right then and there, that he must avoid Miss Eugie Winter for the remainder of the house party. He could not afford to kiss her again.

Ruin was far too dear a cost these days. Especially when he was about to lose everything he had left unless he married.

And fast.

Chapter Six

THE HOUR WAS late.

Eugie could not sleep.

One lone word had been pressing upon her shoulders with the weight of a boulder ever since Grace had interrupted her reckless interlude with the Earl of Hertford earlier in the day: *ruin*.

What a silly notion it was, that ladies could be forever tainted by one action. One word. One lie.

Though she had donned a dressing gown over her night rail, it was most unseemly to be wandering in the night, alone, at a house party, in a state of dishabille. But no amount of turning over in her bed, fluffing her pillow, stoking the fire, or pacing the floor had enabled her to fall into the waiting arms of slumber. She was too hot. Then too cold. There were too many coverlets on her bed. There were not enough.

She was vexed with Lord Hertford. But she still wanted to kiss him.

The only distraction which could save her, she was certain, was a book. Surely there was one to be had in the massive library. She rounded a bend in the corridor and ran into a wall.

A wall of muscle.

That smelled deliciously of soap and man and the Earl of Hertford.

Large hands grasped her arms in a gentle, yet firm, hold. Her palms flattened over a sturdy chest that was covered in the unmistakable lawn of a shirt. When her touch moved higher, she encountered hot, bare flesh and a soft smattering of hair.

His shirt was open.

He wore no cravat.

She was touching his chest.

Realizing the impropriety of the situation—and recalling she was angry with him—she attempted to draw away with such haste, she tripped over one of his feet and nearly went sprawling to the floor.

Hertford had quick reflexes, even in the lack of light, and he caught her, holding her to him.

"Steady," he said, his voice low and delicious.

The rumble of it beneath her fingertips was temptation incarnate. Much like the man himself. Why did he have to smell so wonderful? Why did he have to be so solid and masculine?

"Forgive me my clumsiness," she murmured, reluctant to extricate herself as the reminder of the word which had sent her fleeing from her chamber echoed in her mind once more.

Ruin.

There was so much at stake.

For her brother. For her sisters. For Eugie herself.

She should go. Turn and flee back to the safety of her chamber. But doing wrong had never been so tempting. Never so alluring. Sin had a face and a name, and it was the beautiful Earl of Hertford, enrobed in darkness.

"Eugie?" he asked, surprise coloring his voice. "I ought to have known it would be you."

She was dismayed she had recognized him in the dearth of light when he had failed to do the same with her. "What do you mean, you ought to have known it would be me? I will have you know, I make no habit of wandering about in the night."

"You had damned well better not," he growled.

He sounded frustrated. The same way she felt. All the emotions and sensations rioting within her were heightened in the inkiness of the night, alone with the earl, his male warmth seeping into her.

"Why?" she whispered, a new, distinctly unwise ribbon of daring unfurling within her.

His hands were gliding over her lower back now, moving in a slow seduction she had no desire to stay. "A lady should never go wandering in the night. She could cross paths with the wrong man."

She tipped her head back, trying to find the familiar planes and angles of his face. But there were no windows in this interior hall, no silver moonlight to aid her. She wanted his lips. His mouth was near enough, his breath fanned over hers in the fleeting promise of a kiss.

"Are you the wrong man, my lord?" she asked, keeping her voice low and hushed.

Anyone could come upon them at any moment.

Somehow, the knowledge made molten warmth pool between her thighs. Her body felt heavy and languorous, weighed down by desire. Her hands traveled too, tracing the strength and breadth of his shoulders. He was not wearing a coat or waistcoat. Nothing to separate him from her save the fine lawn of his shirt.

"Every bit as much as you are the wrong woman," he rasped.

She reminded herself she owed him a harangue. That he believed the worst of her. He believed the baron's lies were the truth. But somehow, not even that could keep her caress from wandering up his neck, or her fingers from sinking into his hair. It was silky and thick.

His head lowered.

Her lips parted.

He already believed her ruined. What was the harm in one more kiss? Just one. If she was to continue with her plan of ferreting out the suitors with sinful intentions from amongst the gentlemen in attendance, surely she could kiss the earl and then walk away, finding the library as had been her initial intention.

That was what she told herself until the moment his mouth slanted over hers. Until he took her lips with such possessive intensity, everything inside her melted. The resistance. All the ire. Even the pride, gone. All of it. And she was kissing him back, and his tongue was in her mouth, and her ability to think anything vanished.

There was only hunger.

Need.

Desperation.

In her hands, in his. They turned as one, until her back was against the wall, and his big, hard body held her there, his willing captive. He dragged his mouth down her throat. "Go back to your chamber, Eugie."

The directive was as dark as the night. Tinged with danger. But with promise too, and it was the latter she heeded.

She grasped his hair. It was longer than it had felt beneath her gloves, softer too. The shape of his head seemed perfect beneath her wandering fingers. His mouth opened on her skin, his teeth gently nipping the vee of her shoulder and neck, just where her night rail's prim collar ended.

"Perhaps you should go…" Her words trailed off when his thigh wedged itself between hers.

Instinctively, she rocked against him, and the sensation that exploded in her core was so intense, she could not resist moving again. Her dressing gown parted. Her night rail was a barrier she did not want. Too much fabric between her body and that rigid, warm thigh.

But she did not have long to worry, for his hand grasped a fistful of fabric, lifting it higher. Cool air kissed her bare calf, her knee, and then a hot hand glided over her skin, chasing the cold, making her flesh pebble with awareness. A shiver ran through her that had nothing to do with the December night and everything to do with the man set upon devouring her.

She loved his hands on her. His scent surrounding her. Loved how firm he was. All the places where he was so different from her: his strong arms, his taut abdomen, the coarse stubble of whiskers on his jaw. The contrast between man and woman had never before been so delicious. So decadent.

Why had she been determined to harangue him? Why had she promised Grace she would not kiss him again?

She could not recall. She did not care. Eugie was coming to life in the shadows, her body awakened in a way it never before had. The ache between her thighs became a steady throb. Her breasts felt heavy, her nipples tightening into hardened buds. The friction of her night rail against them felt wicked and wonderful as she moved. She wanted him to touch her there.

And then, the worst part of her imagined what it would be like for him to use his mouth upon her aching flesh. The thought made her hungry, but not in a sense she had ever known before. It made her ache for the maleness of him. All his sharpness and hard edges. His ridges and strength. She knew enough from her discussions with Lady Emilia and the naughty books Christabella had obtained that she understood what happened when a man and woman were intimate.

He would put himself inside her. And she wanted that. It

was the reason for the ache, the hollowness which needed to be filled. She moved over his thigh, seeking relief. Seeking something only he could give.

"Eugie." Her name was part groan. Half prayer.

In his decadent baritone, it rumbled with carnality. She felt like a goddess. And he was worshiping at her altar. Touching her, leaving fire in his wake. The knot holding her dressing gown in place loosened. The garment gaped, and then her hem went higher still, while his nimble fingers worked the buttons on the modest neckline of her night rail. One by one they slid from their moorings. His lips chased each new inch of skin he revealed, kissing down her throat, past her collarbone.

His thigh moved, and she mourned the loss of him between her legs until his hand was there, his fingers delving into her tender flesh where she hungered for him most.

Two gasps rent the night, one his, one hers.

"You're drenched, darling."

And she was. And he had called her *darling*. He did not mean it. She did not care. His blunt-tipped fingers parted her and made the most astounding revelation: a place on her body capable of more pleasure than she had imagined existed. He found a particularly sensitive spot, swirling a caress over it that made her knees give out and a sob flee her lips.

He was there to catch her. To kiss her. To swallow her cry and keep her from falling to the floor. She kissed him back, clutching him with all the desire flooding her. Until she felt him stiffen, and he tore his mouth away.

A low curse fell between them.

"What—"

He pressed a finger over her lips, stilling her words. "Hush. I heard a door open. Footsteps. Come."

Somehow, her fingers connected with his, and they interlaced just before he began tugging her wildly through the hall. She hoped he knew where he was going better than she. A creak in the hall somewhere behind them alerted her they were not alone. Her heart was pounding, her body peculiarly alive with a combination of fear and desire.

In a blink, they reached a door with a thin slat of light glowing beneath it. He hauled it open and pulled her over the threshold, closing the door quickly, almost soundlessly. She stood at his side, their fingers still entwined. In the warm glow of the brace of candles left burning in the chamber, she could not help but to admire the figure he cut. He was taller than most gentlemen, with long legs encased in breeches. In nothing but his white shirt, he looked almost raffish.

Like a highwayman of old.

"Hertford," she began, but he hushed her with a finger to her lips.

Beyond the door, the unmistakable creak of footsteps sounded down the hall.

Someone else was definitely awake despite the lateness of the hour. And that particular someone else was wandering the halls. Which meant their chances of getting caught were greatly increased.

Still, she did not care for the manner in which he had silenced her. Perhaps it was the revelation of their encounter in the hall, perhaps it was the lack of sleep making her bold. She did not know. But the pad of his finger remained firmly upon the center of her lips.

So she did the only thing she could think of doing as she stood in a chamber—Lord knew whose it was, but she hoped it was his—thoroughly kissed, half-undressed, and teeming with unanswered desire.

She licked his finger.

His attention had been toward the door, but she had all of

it now. That hazel gaze was upon her. Searing her. At last, she had what the murk had denied her: the masculine beauty of his face. She could not look away.

And then, her tongue darted out once more. The taste of him was musky. His eyes grew hooded. The air between them was once more filled with tension, rather like the summer sky before a bolt of lightning tore across the stormy blue.

His finger slipped past her lips, into her mouth. She sucked on it.

A low sound emerged from him. "Do you taste yourself?" he whispered.

Surely this was the height of wickedness. She was alone with the Earl of Hertford, his finger in her mouth, the same finger he had used to pleasure her in the hall. The muskiness on his skin was hers.

She ought to be disgusted. Ashamed. Shocked.

But his eyes were burning into hers, and he withdrew his finger from her mouth, then used the wetness of her saliva to paint over her lower lip. "You should not be here."

No, she should not. She should not have done any number of things with this man. Kissed him. Been alone with him. Allowed him to lift her skirts. To touch her intimately. To believe the worst of her, which he still surely did. Somehow, it did not matter that much, not with longing coursing through her veins, wickedness making her weak, her heart pounding, her body aflame. Not when he was near, when her ability to think dissipated.

With great effort, she reminded herself he thought she was ruined. He thought the rumors which had been spread about her were true. But then, she remembered, so did half of London.

"Whose chamber is this?" she asked instead of stopping him. Instead of putting an end to this madness.

"Mine," he told her softly, his finger still gliding from left to right over her lip, his gaze yet burning into hers.

His.

Which meant no one would interrupt them.

Which meant…

Danger.

Temptation.

"I should go," she whispered.

"You should wait," he countered. "Whoever is moving about in the halls could return at any moment."

He stepped closer to her.

She met him. Their bodies collided. And then he was cupping her jaw, kissing her sweetly. Tenderly. Deeper. He licked past the seam of her lips, running his tongue along hers.

Eugie's arms wound around his neck. She was not going anywhere. Did not want to. Her tongue ran against his. They were moving again, but this time it was not toward a wall. It was toward the rumpled bed her frantic eyes had spotted in the shadows.

She knew it. Did not stop it. In fact, she wanted it.

All her life, she had lived in the shadow of being a Winter. Wealthy but reviled. Scorned for her name rather than who she was. And later, thanks to the baron, scorned for lies he had invented to humiliate her after she had denied his suit.

But here she was, the wickedest of the Winters, desired by an earl. The reasons were all wrong, but the desire was not. The desire was real and strong and overwhelming. And so, when they traveled all the way to his bed, and when the backs of her thighs connected with the giving edge of the mattress, she did not protest, because it—he—was what she wanted.

His kisses, his touch, *him*. Everything. Whatever it would mean.

The Earl of Hertford had the most unusual ability to set

her aflame, and she did not want it to end. Not his touch. Not his kiss. Not this night.

They were still kissing as they fell to the bed together. He braced himself over her on his forearms, keeping the full weight of his body from slamming into her with their undignified landing. She giggled up at him, linked her arms around his neck, and then the time for levity was done.

His mouth swooped back down on hers. He kissed her as if he could not resist, as if he needed to drink from her lips. It was a union of tongues and mouths, the scrape of teeth. Primal. Powerful.

A new wave of sensation hit her, like the crashing furor of the ocean in the midst of a maelstrom. Dev had taken them all to Brighton once, and a storm had been brewing, which had rendered bathing in the ocean entirely impossible. But watching the waves had been beautiful. Shocking. Life at its rawest and fullest capacity.

Which was how she felt now, in this moment. She was a tempest which had been brewing for years. The Earl of Hertford was the powder keg that had been sparked into flame. And she was burning for him. Alight and so very alive.

Either she would douse his flames, or he would burn her up, for they were not meant for each other. She knew it. He had said it. And yet, they could not resist each other. She could not return to her chamber as she ought. And she could not stop touching him, kissing him.

But she was in good company, for neither could he.

Somehow, they wrestled her free of her dressing gown while she was still on her back. Then his shirt, too, was gone, pulled over his head and tossed to the floor. His chest was a revelation. In the soft glow of the light, she could at last see what she had felt in the hall. Dark springs of curls dotted his chest. His muscles were clearly delineated bands on his abdomen.

She ran her hand up and down his bare chest, absorbing every sinew, every rigid slab. He was warm and smooth and vital, his body tensing beneath her questing touch.

Wrong had never felt so deliciously, wickedly right.

Chapter Seven

*C*AM HAD TO stop kissing Miss Eugie Winter.

He *would* stop kissing her, he promised himself. After just one more. And another.

Soon.

Or perhaps later. What was the harm in lingering with her just a bit longer? In allowing just a few more liberties after so many boundaries had been crossed between them, not just this night but on previous occasions?

Besides, she felt far too good in his arms. Far too right in his bed. Her lips were made for his, and they were currently kissing him back with all the need firing his blood. Her tongue touched his, and he was nearly gone. About to spend into his breeches like a callow lad.

He forgot about propriety. Ignored the rules. He had devoted his life to living above reproach. He had cultivated his reputation. Had never brought one moment of shame upon his mother, upon himself.

Why, then, should he utterly lose control now? It made no sense, the power this woman had over him. The power to change him, to make him want to take every risk just to keep her here in his arms, in his bed, her lips and body beneath his just a bit longer…

It was dangerous, to be sure. She was temptation incarnate.

Her body beneath his was supple and welcoming, her thighs bracketing his. She was learning his bare chest, setting him aflame. Her small hands, her delicate fingers, the tentative yet sure manner in which she touched him… *Christ*, it was enough to make him lose himself.

His ballocks were already drawn tight, his cock rigid against the fall of his breeches from their encounter in the hall. The way she had moved on his thigh, coating his breeches with her dew.

He groaned into her mouth as he kissed her. *Bloody hell*, he would never forget the night he had met Miss Eugie Winter in a darkened hall and had nearly taken her then and there.

He wanted to take her now.

God, how he wanted.

But he knew he must not.

He would stop this madness.

Except his hands seemed to have a mind of their own. They wanted what they wanted. Eugie's skin. They fisted in her night rail, and then pulled it up. She writhed beneath him, helping him to draw the diaphanous fabric over her head. And then she was naked in his bed.

Her breasts were even larger than they had looked, trapped in the confines of her bodice. Pale and round. Her nipples were hard little buds prodding the air like offerings. He lowered his head, drew one between his lips, and sucked. The moan that left her sent another arrow of need to his cock.

He flicked his tongue over her, swirled it around the peak of her breast, as if he had all night to savor her. Which he did not. And this was wrong. He must put an end to it. The Earl of Hertford did not dally with unwed females. He bedded seasoned courtesans. He avoided scandal.

His hand craved the velvet softness of Eugie's curves. He

found her other nipple, nipping it with his teeth, as his fingers dipped into her folds. She was wetter than she had been in the hall, her essence coating him, taunting him. He teased her pearl, petting it in light strokes until she jerked against his hand, straining for more.

He whispered her name as he kissed a path down her belly, worshiping her body. "Eugie." A sigh, a plea.

Desperation and need mingled.

Wrong. This was so very wrong. But he had lost control. And now, he was between the smooth curves of her hips. He could see her—all of her—glistening pink flesh beneath a smattering of curls. The pouty plumpness of her clitoris. The cove he wanted to claim as his own.

He settled his mouth upon her there, suckling her as he had done to her nipple. The taste of her blossomed on his tongue, the sweetness of the most exotic fruit mingled with the spicy musk of woman. Her gasp told him she liked what he was doing, so he sucked harder, then ran his tongue down her seam. He licked into her cunny, gratified when she moaned and thrust against him.

All the blood in his body was roaring to his cock. He had never wanted anything so badly in his life. Now that he had her beneath him, he could not get enough. Sensation and need overwhelmed him. The taste of her on his tongue, the tiny quivers of her body beneath his, the breathy sounds of contentment she made, almost kittenish. It was so much.

Too much.

More than he had bargained for.

He could not stop now until he was inside her. Until he had claimed her. Until she was his. Just for the night. For this night. He made love to her with his mouth, inhaling deeply of her scent, finding a place with his tongue that seemed particularly sensitive and abrading it lightly with the whiskers of his jaw. When he sucked on her pearl again, she went rigid beneath him, crying out as she spent.

He should have been concerned about the loudness of her voice in the night, coming from his chamber. But he was past the point of caring about anything other than her pleasure. As she came on his tongue, he glanced up her body, over the gentle swell of her belly, past the mounds of her breasts, to her face. Her head was thrown back in ecstasy, eyes closed tight, lips open, back arched.

His desire for her was like a beast, overtaking him. Clouding his mind. Drowning out the part of him that had lived a life dedicated to always doing the right thing. He was going to do the wrong thing now. Just once.

He was going to take her.

He had to.

Cam rose between her legs, on his knees, fingers fumbling to tear open the fall of his breeches. In his haste to flee his chamber earlier, he had foregone his smalls. His cock sprang free, swelled, thick, and ready. He felt, at once, as if he had been waiting a lifetime for this moment. Which was strange, since he scarcely knew her but a few days.

"Eugie." Her name was torn from him again, and the longing in his own voice cut him like the blade of a dagger.

He dragged his cock through her slippery folds, asking a question he had no right to pose. He told himself she was experienced. No innocent miss would kiss as she had. No innocent miss would be so eager for assignations. She had done this before. With Cunningham, and though the thought made him want to smash his fist into the baron's thin blade of a nose, he banished it from his mind.

There was no place for others here between them. There was only passion.

"Do you want this?" He held himself still, waiting for her

answer.

THERE WAS ONLY one word that would form on her lips.

"Yes," she told him.

Whatever *this* was, she wanted it. With him.

She was going to give her body to the Earl of Hertford. Her virginity as well. She should be ashamed of herself. She should put an end to it before they went too far. But something had changed. *She* had changed. It was as if the journey down the hall in the darkness had made her into someone else.

All her life, she had always listened to her brother. She had never been reckless like her sister Bea, never longing for romance like Christabella. She was the one who felt too much, who had worn her heart on her sleeve until it had been ruthlessly broken.

But she did not want to be that Eugie any longer.

She wanted to be the Eugie who was naked in the Earl of Hertford's bed, the woman he worshiped with his hands and mouth. The one he wanted.

His jaw was rigid as he looked down at her, his hazel eyes taking her breath in the warm glow of the candlelight. The cords in his neck were tense. His strong arms were flexed, and she could see so much of him, so many delicious details: the shadow of whiskers on his chin, the whorls of hair on his chest, the veins in his upper arms, the taut ridges of his abdomen.

"Are you certain?" he asked, his baritone part growl, part silken seduction.

It made her shiver.

"Yes," she said again, but then something occurred to her.

She did not know his Christian name, and they were as intimate as man and woman could be, flesh on flesh, his body about to join hers. "What shall I call you?"

"Cam," he gritted.

"Cam," she repeated.

She liked the sound of it, the shortness of it. She liked the way he looked, his big body dominating hers, her legs spread, his manhood protruding from his opened breeches. He took himself in hand as she watched, gripping the long, rigid length. How beautiful it was, that part of him, and she wanted to touch it. Would have, had he not settled himself against her and thrust it inside.

One pump of his hips. She tensed at the invasion, at the unexpected feeling of it. He was too large. Or she was too small. There was a burning pinch, a throb.

He held himself still, staring down at her with a strange expression on his face. "You are a virgin."

Of course she was. *Had been.* What had he thought? What had she expected him to think, with her brazen behavior?

Shame swirled through her, chasing the pleasure. "Cam," she began.

"I am sorry," he said. "I have never… Have I hurt you?"

Yes.

"No," she lied. What hurt the most was on the inside. Her heart. Or perhaps her pride.

"Let me make it better," he said.

She wondered how he could.

But then, his mouth was on her. He was sucking her nipples, and his touch moved between them to stroke her. He moved slowly, withdrawing, sliding through the slickness of her channel. The pleasure returned. Desire was a knot, building, tangling her up.

He thrust again, pressing deeper, and the pain dimmed. The discomfort was replaced by only a wondrous fullness. The sensation of him inside her was nothing short of exquisite.

His mouth was on her neck again, sucking. Devouring her as if she were the finest sweet. His breaths were harsh and hot on her skin. She gave in to the sensation, to the pleasure. Everything else fled. There was only the two of them, moving as one. She learned how to undulate her hips beneath him, chasing more, chasing the pleasure building to a new crescendo.

Her release slammed into her with a force that had her body bowing, her head back. A cry was on her lips, and then his mouth was on hers, swallowing the cry. His tongue was slipping inside, tasting her as his body continued to slide in and out of hers. Faster now. The thrill of it licked down her spine. She tasted herself on his mouth. On his tongue.

As the last of her spasms subsided, he jerked himself from her body, gripped his shaft, and spent his seed into the bedclothes. There was blood on his hand, faint traces of it on his manhood. Hers, she realized as he rolled to his back at her side.

She felt alive as she never had before. Her body ached and tingled in strange places. Her breaths were ragged and harsh. Languor stole over her, and she was suddenly drowsy. He gathered her to his side, pressed a kiss to the top of her head in a tender gesture that pricked her heart.

But then he said the last words she wanted to hear.

"I am sorry, Eugie."

Her head was nestled on his chest, above his madly thumping heart. He was warm and reassuring, his massive frame curved around hers despite their state of undress. She realized he was still wearing his breeches.

The confusion on his face as he had entered her returned,

as did the telltale manner in which he had stiffened. The disbelieving tone in his voice when he had uttered the most damning words of all. *You are a virgin.*

As if he had expected her to be a well-practiced courtesan.

"You believed the rumors," she said.

She knew it was true, but part of her needed to hear his confirmation. The words from his lips. The scent of him and their lovemaking was rich in the air, somehow a comfort and a reproach at the same time.

The silence was damning.

"Eugie—"

"No," she cut him off, lifting her head from the warmth of his chest because she knew she must. She had been foolish with him. More foolish than she had been with the baron. More foolish than she had ever been.

The regret on his countenance hit her like a blow.

"I am sorry," he said again.

But she did not want his apologies.

She scrambled from the bed, acutely aware of her nudity, searching for her night rail. It had been tossed to the floor in a heap. Somehow, it was the sight of that white linen discarded upon the carpet, more than the blood she had shed, which made her realize she had just lost her maidenhead to a man she scarcely knew.

To a man who had believed the worst of her.

How stupid she was. She snatched it up and threw it over her head, dashing away more proof of her foolishness with the back of her hand. Tears: hot, humiliating. She could not stop them.

"Eugie." He had risen from the bed without her taking note, and his hand was on her back now, tracing her spine in a caress.

She stepped away from him, whirling. "Do not touch

me."

"We will marry, of course," he said, staring at her, standing there clad in nothing but his breeches, unfairly beautiful. "I will go to your brother in the morning and ask for your hand."

"No," she snapped at him. "We will not. And you will not."

Dev would kill him. And her. She did not say all that, however. Because she could not say anything. Her emotions were choking her. Her tears were embarrassing her.

She did not wait for his response. Did not bother to retrieve her dressing gown. She simply fled.

Chapter Eight

$\mathcal{C}$AM WOKE TO the scent of Eugie on his sheets. To the reminder of his folly vividly represented in the specks of her blood mottling the bed linens.

And to a hard cock.

Because he was a beast.

A stupid, rutting beast.

He had lost control. He had become no better than his father. Had betrayed his sense of right and wrong. Had taken Eugie's innocence. Something he had no right to claim. And he wanted to do it now all over again.

Lord God, the feeling of being deep inside her body. She had been so tight, so wet. He could still feel the heat of her. The trace of his tongue over his lower lip revealed he could still taste her, too.

He passed a hand over his face, groaning in misery. He had been wrong about her. Some part of him had known it before he had torn through her maidenhead. Before the cloud of hurt darkening her eyes when she had made the realization of just how much of an ass he was.

He had merely been so greedy, so selfish in his desire for her, he had not listened to the voice of reason. Her response to him had inflamed him. She did not kiss like a virgin. He had told himself a virgin would not permit the liberties he had taken.

He realized now what a blockhead he had been. He had never kissed a virgin. Had never done more than dance with one, beneath the glittering chandeliers of a society ball and the watchful eyes of mamas and chaperones. How the bloody hell would he know how they kissed? What they allowed?

Why had he taken her without the binds of matrimony?

And why did it have to be *her*, the Winter most embroiled in scandal?

He knew why. Because there was something about her that called to him in a way no other woman before her had. He had seen her, and he had wanted her. That night at the ball, he had thought she had looked like an invitation to sin, and he had been right. But it was more than that, if he were honest.

More than her generous breasts, her luscious curves, her sweet lips, her beauty.

It was Eugie.

And she had left a part of her behind in his bed. His hand settled in her dressing gown now, grasping the soft fabric as if seeking her warmth, as if chasing the feel of her. He raised it to his nose before he could stop himself and inhaled deeply. There it was, the scent of fragrant summer blossoms. Her skin had smelled of it everywhere.

Ah, her silken, creamy skin. Her legs.

Still holding her dressing gown, he threw back the bed-clothes with his free hand and rose. He had not been the same ever since he had cast his eye upon a goddess in a red gown. And he could not pluck her from his mind now. She was nothing he should want, and all he desired.

He was going to make her his countess.

There was no question of it, in spite of her denial last night. In spite of her reputation, which he now had firsthand knowledge was a blatant falsehood. He had made a fine muck of things. But he would seek out Eugie at the first possible opportunity. He had to make this right.

Without further harm to the lady in question.

Which meant he had a dressing gown to hide and some bed linens to dispose of.

And then, he had a lot of thinking to do.

A KNOCK SOUNDED at Eugie's chamber door, and for a fleeting foolish moment she thought it was him.

The Earl of Hertford.

Cam.

The man she had lain with last night. Who she had given her maidenhead.

Her fists clenched on the counterpane, and she pulled it protectively to her chin. She did not want to see him. Did not want to look at him. Because if she did, her defenses would crumble. If she did, she would recall every blazing moment of what had happened between them last night.

That was a lie.

She was already thinking of it. Had not stopped, all through the hours she had lain awake in the darkness, nor all the hours since she had risen after finally falling into a fitful slumber. How could she forget?

Everything had changed for her in a glorious, life-altering way, and yet she was terrified. Because the earl wanted to marry her. And she suspected she knew why…

The door opened and her sister-in-law, the elegant Lady Emilia, appeared. Her lovely face was pinched with concern as she closed the door at her back and crossed the chamber.

"Eugie," she said softly as she settled on the side of the bed. "What is the matter?"

Eugie had asked for her breakfast to be delivered to her chamber this morning, not ready yet to face the gathering. To face her sisters, Lady Emilia, her brother.

To face the earl.

"I have my courses," she lied. "I am feeling rather ill. Forgive me for not attending breakfast. I know you have gone to great lengths to organize this house party for the sake of me and my sisters."

And I have ruined it and myself.

Emilia's gaze slipped to Eugie's throat. "Are you certain that is the real reason you avoided the breakfast table?"

A gnawing sense of worry overtook her. "Yes, of course it is."

"I have some pearl powder which ought to serve you well," Lady Emilia said solemnly. "Or perhaps a fichu, placed just right."

Her dread grew. "I am afraid I do not understand. How can a fichu or a powder remedy a female complaint?"

Her sister-in-law's lips compressed as she eyed her with a frank stare. "You have distinct marks on your throat, my dear. From a man's whiskers. That is why you are hiding here, is it not?"

Dear heavens. She had not ventured to look in the glass this morning. She had simply been too distraught over her recklessness, too hurt that everything she had feared about the earl had been true. Hiding, it was true. Hiding from Hertford, from what they had done together.

Hiding from the horrible suspicion which had occurred to her by the grim light of dawn, when she had jolted awake in her bed. The suspicion that the earl had not bedded her because he had believed Cunningham's vicious lies about her, but rather because he, too was a fortune hunter.

Only, he had succeeded where the baron had failed. He

had compromised her in deed and not just word. His proposal had been instant. It had not been a question, but a statement. She had to discover if he was in need of a wealthy bride just as the baron had been.

"Eugie," her sister-in-law prodded gently. "That is the reason, yes?"

Mortified heat flared in her cheeks. "I do not wish to have this conversation with you," she stammered at last, hating the penetrating stare her brother's wife had leveled upon her, which seemed to see far too much.

"Would you prefer to have it with me or with your brother?" Emilia asked.

Though her voice remained soft and concerned, there was an edge hiding behind it. Her sister-in-law was gentle and kind, but fierce when need be.

"You know I would rather have it with you," she forced herself to respond.

Dev was a wonderful brother, always putting the needs of his sisters first, but he was also exceedingly protective. She shuddered to think what would happen if he discovered the truth of what had occurred the night before. He and Hertford would tear each other apart. Though her brother was large and strong, so, too was the earl. It was difficult to determine which of them would emerge the victor, and it was a battle she had no wish to see.

"Then you must be honest with me, Eugie," Emilia said now. "I cannot help you if you are hiding the truth from me."

She did not dare tell her sister-in-law the full extent of her folly, did she? No, she did not. She was not certain if she could tell anyone. If she could bear to form the words.

Where to begin?

"What do you know of the Earl of Hertford?" she asked, for her alarm had only continued to grow.

The small seed of doubt had already taken root and sprouted. But she would not be trapped. She would sooner spend the rest of her days hidden away in shame first.

Emilia frowned. "Is he the one?"

"Please." She closed her eyes for a moment, battling her emotions. Her heart was as sore as her body, aching in all the places he had claimed. "Just tell me…is he pockets to let?"

Her sister-in-law's expression grew pained. "His father, the former earl, was a notorious wastrel."

Everything inside her froze. "He would need to wed a wealthy bride, then, would he not?"

"Yes, I would suspect it, but why, Eugie?" Emilia searched her gaze. "Surely Hertford cannot be the man responsible for the marks on your throat? One of the reasons I chose to invite him is that he has always been above reproach as a gentleman. His sobriquet is the Prince of Proper."

He had most certainly not been the Prince of Proper last night.

Her ears went hot as she recalled what he had done to her, his tongue between her legs, his manhood inside her. And to her shame, a dull throb pounded to life at her core. A traitorous ache that told her she would gladly have more of the pleasure he had given. Despite what she had just learned about him.

Foolish, foolish body. Stupid, wounded heart.

"It was not the earl," she lied. "It was another."

"Who, if not Hertford?" Emilia asked shrewdly.

"I would prefer not to say." She paused. "I promise it will not happen again."

"I am afraid your promise is not good enough, Eugie." Her sister-in-law sighed. "You are my sister now, and I love you. I want to protect you. I cannot do that if you do not tell me what happened and with whom."

She knew Emilia was right. Still, she could not bear to reveal the full extent of what had happened. "It was reckless and unwise on my part, and I am so sorry for my actions. But please, Emilia, do not make me tell you the name of the gentleman. It was a mistake which shall not be repeated. I promise you."

"Did the gentleman in question force you?" Emilia pressed. "If you were coerced or manhandled, your brother must hear of it at once."

"No," she reassured her sister-in-law. "My foolishness was purely voluntary. A moment alone, and I gave in to my weakness. It was a few kisses, nothing more. As I said, it shan't be repeated."

"It *cannot* be repeated," Emilia warned gently. "You understand that, do you not, my dear? We are working so hard to restore your reputation after what that regrettable little toad did to you. We cannot afford to cause a scandal. It will affect not only you, but your sisters as well. Promise me you will not do something so reckless again, Eugie."

She closed her eyes once more, unable to look at the kindness on Emilia's face any longer, knowing she was lying to her sister-in-law, knowing just how great a scandal was already in the making.

"I promise," she whispered, guilt curdling in her gut and making her misery complete.

She would do everything in her power to hold true to that promise.

Everything.

ONE FACT WAS becoming painfully apparent to Cam: Miss Eugie Winter was avoiding him.

Not just avoiding him. *Hiding* from him.

An entire day had gone by without a single sighting of her. And he had looked for her. Everywhere. All whilst attempting not to be too obvious in his search. He had not asked after her directly, for fear his interest would become suspect. She had not been present at breakfast, nor for any of the festive afternoon diversions occupying his fellow guests. Dinner, too, had come and gone without her.

This morning, he was once again riding with Aylesford at his side, hoping the chill of the bitter December air would give him some much-needed clarity on what he needed to do. Thus far, it had not.

"You look remarkably grim," his friend noted, his breath making wisps of fog as he spoke.

"As do you," he observed. "I have yet to hear word of your betrothal."

It was a relief to settle upon the problems of someone else, at least for a moment. Distracting himself from thoughts of Eugie was proving more difficult by the hour.

"That is because I have yet to secure the acquiescence of my betrothed," Aylesford noted, his jaw tensing as he made the admission. "She says she is not certain she wishes to be tied to a scoundrel such as me even in a feigned courtship. Do you believe the airs of the minx?"

Perhaps the viscount had met his match in Miss Grace Winter.

"Your reputation *is* black," he pointed out.

"More like dun," Aylesford argued.

"And you *are* a scoundrel," he continued, ignoring his friend's interjection.

Then again, so was he. What manner of gentleman stole a lady's innocence in the midst of a house party? Or *ever*, for that matter?

"I am not a scoundrel." Aylesford scowled at him. "Devil take it, Hertford, whose side are you on?"

"Yours, of course," he said, bracing himself against a sudden, cold gust of wind. "Which is why I am pointing out how the lady must feel about things."

He could have been speaking to himself.

Indeed, he *was* speaking to himself.

And he realized how much of a cad he must seem to Eugie. Or perhaps—worse—a fortune hunter. Which he was. Both of those things. Yes, he was.

"The lady is not required to have feelings on the matter," Aylesford was saying. "The vexing wench is proving more difficult to woo as a feigned betrothed than a true betrothed would be. If I actually wished to marry her—which I most assuredly do not—I would simply go to her brother and ask the devil for her hand. It would be as simple as that."

"Why do you not do that?" he asked his friend, and once more, the question was one he should be asking himself as well. "Go to Mr. Winter directly. It is hardly a secret he is attempting to secure noble husbands for his sisters. I should think he would be more than happy to accept your suit."

Mayhap he should do the same: approach Mr. Winter. Ask for Eugie's hand.

"I would if I was assured the lady in question would agree to the match," Aylesford grumbled. "But although I have no intention of ever shackling myself to anyone, and she knows it, she may refuse to agree to the feigned betrothal, just to spite me."

True. There was that possibility for him as well. Eugie had been angry with him when she had fled his chamber two nights ago, and with good reason. Cam stared into the field that stretched out before them, wishing he knew what the hell to do next.

Eugie had once more been absent from breakfast. How was he to induce her to give him another chance when he could not find her?

"You will have to persuade her," he told Aylesford.

"Of course I will," the viscount agreed. "But I do not know how."

He was not alone in that sentiment. Cam frowned. "Perhaps you could convince her using the same methods you have employed with others. How do you woo a woman into becoming your mistress, for instance?"

"I have but to look at women and they leap into my bed by the legions," his friend drawled.

Damn Aylesford and his sarcastic wit. "What an extraordinary talent to have," he returned.

"Don't be daft, Hertford." Aylesford gave him a look. "I give them gifts. Baubles. Pay them attention. Smile at them. Nibble at their necks in darkened alcoves. That sort of thing."

"It sounds as if you have been reading Minerva press books." He grinned. "Little wonder you are not having any luck with convincing Miss Winter to be your pretend betrothed."

"Go to the devil," Aylesford told him without heat.

"I rather suspect I already have," he said grimly, thinking of what he had done. How far he had allowed himself to go beyond the bounds of propriety.

He had to make this right.

Somehow.

But first, he had to find Eugie.

"The Prince of Proper?" Aylesford raised a brow. "What could you possibly do that would land you in eternal damnation?"

Kiss an unwed lady senseless in a dark hall. Take her into his chamber. Strip off her dressing gown and night rail…

From there, he had to stop his thoughts.

Because they were decidedly wicked. And wrong. And it was a hell of a thing to sport an erection whilst one was riding a horse with Viscount Aylesford as company.

"All manner of sins," was all he said.

But he was going to atone.

And to do so, it was becoming apparent to him he had only one choice: sneak into Eugie's chamber and confront her, face-to-face.

Chapter Nine

*H*IS TONGUE WAS *in her mouth, and his hands were traveling all over her body. Cupping her breasts, playing with her nipples until they hardened into distended peaks. Lower, following the curve of her waist down to her hips. And then, his fingers touched her. Where she was wet for him, throbbing for him, aching for him.*

She moaned into his kiss, writhing against him.

This was all wrong.

He was *all wrong.*

And yet, she never wanted it to end.

A decadent spiral of desire was twisting through her, making her every sense more potent and powerful. He worked over her flesh harder. Faster.

But still it was not enough. She wanted more...

"Eugie."

"Go away," she muttered, half-asleep, trying to get back to the place she had been, on the brink of the most delirious, mind-shattering climax.

"Eugie." There was the voice again, deep and delicious.

His voice.

Slowly, her eyes opened, blinking into the darkened chamber. Surely, it had been a dream. Surely, the Earl of Hertford was not truly in her room. She turned her head on the pillow and let out a shriek when she found him standing beside her bed, illuminated by the flickering glow of a small brace of tapers.

"Damnation," he muttered, scowling at her. "No screaming unless you want the entire wing at your door demanding to know what is going on in here, and then you will truly have no choice but to wed me."

Her body was instantly aware of his nearness. Undoubtedly the dream she had been having about him did not help matters. Her nipples were hard. Her skin was flushed. Why, oh why, did she have to be so responsive to the scoundrel?

She clutched the bedclothes to her neck as if they were a shield. "What are you doing in my chamber?"

"Lower your voice, Eugie." He settled his rump upon the edge of her bed.

"Get off my bed!" she whispered furiously.

"I need to be nearer to you so no one will overhear us," he returned.

"The only thing you need to do is go away," she countered.

"I want to speak with you." His low voice was as delicious as ever, sending an unwanted trill through her.

She ignored it. "Speak with me elsewhere."

"I would have." His jaw clenched. "But you have been hiding away in here for two days. I had no choice but to come to you."

"I am not hiding." Her cheeks went hot. "I am ill."

A shadow flickered over his face. "Is it because of me? Because of that night? You are not in pain, are you?"

Only internal agony, but she was not going to admit that to him.

"No," she snapped. "Now do get out of my chamber, Lord Hertford. You do not belong in here, and if this is some sort of stunt to entrap me into marriage, I can assure you, I will not go through with it. I will not be forced into marriage with a fortune-hunting cad. One man tried it before you, and he was not any more successful than you will be."

His nostrils flared. "I am not attempting to force you into anything."

"I distinctly recall your words the other night."

"Admittedly, my delivery was lacking. I merely wanted to reassure you I would take care of you."

"I do not *need* to be taken care of," she returned.

"Allow me to rephrase." His tone was as grim as his countenance as he paused. "I wanted to reassure you I would not bed and then refuse to wed you. While my actions have suggested otherwise, and I do not blame you for reaching such a conclusion, I am a man of honor."

"And why would I wish to wed any man, least of all you?" she demanded, still unimpressed by his efforts.

Dev could not make her marry anyone.

She could go somewhere, take her disgrace elsewhere. To the deepest, darkest recesses of the country, where no one knew her name and she could not taint her family. She could buy a cottage and plant roses in her garden and live off her fortune and take care of herself.

It did not seem a bad plan.

Perhaps lonely.

She would miss her sisters and her brother, certainly.

But she could do it. She was strong.

"Because you could be carrying my babe," he said then, a fervent note in his voice she had not heard before. "I took measures to ensure my seed would not take root, but nothing is certain."

The dream of the cottage and the roses—the cottage was made of limestone and it overlooked a meadow filled with wildflowers and dotted with the occasional cow—suddenly changed. She imagined herself sitting in a rocking chair, a babe in her arms.

A babe with the Earl of Hertford's blade of a nose and proud chin.

And a strange, new warmth crept over her, from the inside out. Unfurling like the bud of a rose, tightly packed at first, before blossoming into a luscious burst of petals beneath the heat of the sun.

A mother.

She had never before thought of having a child. Of a babe growing in her womb. The prospect was not at all upsetting. Nor, to her dismay, was the thought of the earl as the child's sire.

"Eugie," he prodded, sidling nearer to her on the bed. Near enough he could find her left hand, which had been resting idly in her lap while the right held her bedclothes to her chin.

Their fingers tangled, and his skin was hot and smooth, his touch firm and reassuring. She ought to withdraw.

She did not.

"My babe could be growing within you now," he said.

And she, fool that she was, laced her fingers tighter in his. Just for a moment. Just for a beat. Until she recalled he was a fortune hunter.

She withdrew her hand at last. "It does not signify. I will not wed you, Lord Hertford."

"Cam." His hazel gaze flitted over her face, studying her, searching, it seemed, for something.

She knew not what.

"Lord Hertford," she repeated. "Remove yourself from my bed and from my chamber at once. You are not welcome here."

"I am not going anywhere until you agree to become my countess." His fingers stroked the top of her hand.

She liked the touch too much, so she delivered a sound little smack to him, as if she were a governess and he her naughty charge. "Do stop touching me, Hertford. I do not like it."

A lie.

A blatant, horrible lie.

Because the weakness inside her could not resist this man for long, and she knew it. Which was why he had to get out of her chamber. Out of this wing. Out of Abingdon House altogether, if possible. Far away. She would send him to the moon if she could.

And even then, she would yearn for him.

What was wrong with her? *He is a fortune hunter*, she reminded herself. *Pockets to let. Manipulating you. Making you feel cherished. Bedding you to force your hand. Think of the cottage, the roses.*

She thought of the babe who looked like Cam.

Cam.

Yes, that was how she thought of him now. He had been inside her, after all. He had lain with her and given her pleasure she had never imagined existed. And now, he had invaded her chamber the way he had invaded her body.

"You do not like my touch?" he asked silkily.

And she realized, oh how she realized, that of all the prevarications she could have attempted with this man, she had chosen the worst. For it was a challenge. The gauntlet had been dropped.

There was no retrieving it now. So she tilted up her chin, meeting his gaze, and lied some more. "No."

"Eugie." His deep and delicious voice was knowing.

"I am Miss Winter to you," she corrected. "And you must

go."

He did not go. Instead, he inched nearer. His long, strong leg was hooked at the knee, his breeches drawn tight. She would have been grateful he was fully dressed, wearing shirtsleeves and even a waistcoat and cravat, but for the loving fit of those breeches. She could see all of him.

The sinews of his thigh muscles, earned from riding. The strength of his calf. The bulge of his manhood beneath the falls of his breeches. Long and thick. The memory of how it had felt, sliding inside her, produced a burning throb deep within. He had stretched her, known her body in ways she could have never dreamt.

Naughty books, wicked words, engravings—none of these could compare to the visceral experience of being claimed. And he had done that. *Cam* had done that. He had claimed her. Possessed her.

Filled her.

He was staring at her lips, his gaze hooded. She should not want him as she did. Should not feel the hunger firing to life deep within her. But she did. Something was wrong with her. *He* was wrong with her. Yes, this affliction was all his fault. She would bury herself in the country where he could never find her. Never look at her with those hazel eyes, those well-molded lips.

"Tell me again," he said.

And his voice, his words, they were a dare.

She stared at his mouth, longing to feel it on hers although she knew she should not. "Tell you what, Lord Hertford?"

"To go." He slid closer. She was trapped in the spell of his eyes. His potent maleness. His beauty. "Tell me you do not like my touch."

Her lips were parted. Her sex felt heavy. The throb turned

into an ache. A hunger. The burning within her intensified. His possession of her had been exquisite, a marriage of discomfort and pleasure, terrifying and delicious all at once. The pain had turned into the most flawless thrill.

A thrill she longed for again now.

Dear God, in spite of everything, she wanted him again.

"Tell me," he repeated. "Do it, Eugie. Make those pretty red lips tell me to go."

She stared at him. The words would not come. The strangeness which had overtaken her was potent. Confusing. She felt as she had once when she consumed too much wine. Glowing. Warm. But something more…

Wicked.

Yes, that was it.

Her tongue ran over her lips. "Go."

His expression changed, hardening. He began sliding away. "Very well. If that is what you truly wish, I will—"

"No," she said, too loudly.

The denial rang through her chamber. When it came to the Earl of Hertford, it seemed her foolishness knew no bounds. She flinched from the force of it. From the betrayal, too. Her own voice. Her own tongue. Telling him not to leave. Telling him to stay.

She did not want him to stay. Did she?

Of course not.

Her hand had closed around his wrist like a manacle and she had not realized it. He had, however, for his head was down, his gaze settled upon the connection. The silence that descended was louder than her objection had been, hanging between them. Weighing down the night.

She released him at once.

"You want me to stay, Eugie?" he asked.

The silk had returned to his baritone. The low, seductive

rumble. The velvet wrapped around marble.

"I am not finished with our dialogue," she invented hastily.

"You like my touch."

The certainty in his tone nettled.

Her eyes narrowed. "I never said that."

He was grinning at her now. Sitting on her bed, in the midst of the night, grinning. And looking so handsome he made her ache. "You did not need to say it. I already know. Your lips say it. Your wide eyes. The way your body reacts whenever I touch you."

He was right.

Blast him, he was right.

"Flesh is weak," she said.

"I cannot argue the point." His stare was intense, holding her captive. "I have never felt more incapable of denying myself what I want than when I am in your presence."

She should not ask him, she knew it, and yet his words had sent an arrow of heat through her. "What is it you want, my lord?"

"You." He paused, his countenance turning rueful. "Even though I should not."

"You want my dowry," she corrected. "You are in need of funds, yes?"

"Yes," he startled her by admitting, "I am in desperate need of a wealthy bride."

She had not expected candor from him. But still, she would not be swayed.

"You want to marry me because you require my dowry," she pressed.

"No, Eugie." He inched a bit closer on the bed. "I want to marry you because I made love to you. You could be carrying my babe. Marrying you is the right thing to do."

"I am certain the prospect of assuaging all your troubles with my fortune has nothing at all to do with it," she said drily, forcing herself to remain stern.

His scent and his mouth and his words would not persuade her she was wrong.

"Do you know what I am called?" he asked then, taking her by surprise once more with the sudden change of subjects.

"The Earl of Hertford." She frowned at him, wondering what manner of game he was about now. "And if you move any nearer to me, you shall be called a man with a blackened eye as well."

His lips twitched into a half smile, almost as if he were repressing a burst of laughter. "No, Eugie. My sobriquet. Do you not know what all society calls me?"

Lady Emilia's words returned to her then, swiftly. "The Prince of Proper."

His lips firmed once more, no hint of levity remaining. "Precisely. And do you know why they call me that?"

He was wearing her down, and she knew it. Exploiting her weakness. Her body's incurable yearning for him was playing upon her emotions. She had to remain strong. Unyielding.

"Presumably not because you make a habit of hauling ladies into your chamber at house parties and stealing their innocence," she drawled.

His lips twitched again. "No, I do not make a habit of it. Nor did I *haul* you, as I recall. Someone was coming, and I feared we would be seen."

"It is reassuring to know the rest of the company is not in danger of falling victim to your insatiable carnal appetite," she murmured. "But now, you truly must go, Hertford. I do not care what your sobriquet is or why you have earned it. I will not wed you."

He did not heed her, however. He remained where he was, encroaching upon her bed, his stare riveted upon her. "I am known as the Prince of Proper because I have always taken great care to be above reproach. My father was a scoundrel, forever courting scandal and ruin, and I have lived each day of my life striving to be as different from him as the sun is from the moon."

His revelation affected her, although it should not. His tone, like his expression, was open. Earnest. For all his faults, the Earl of Hertford did not strike her as a liar.

"Thank you for enlightening me," she forced herself to say, determined to remain impervious to him. "Now go, my lord."

"I am not finished," he said firmly but gently. "I am attempting, in my muddled way, to explain to you that what came over me several nights ago was an aberration. It still defies logic and reasoning. I do not despoil innocents. I do not find myself in unwed ladies' chambers."

"It would seem you do," she interjected.

"I do now," he agreed, his sensual lips unsmiling. "Because of you."

"Because of my wealth," she countered. "Pray do not attempt to pretend you want to marry me for any other reason. As I have told you, I will not marry a fortune hunter. I would sooner carry out my life in a cottage in the country, tending roses and forgetting I ever had the bad sense to go into that chamber with you."

"There is no pretense here." His voice was steady. Sure. "There is only truth. I need a wealthy bride, but I do not need *you*. However, I have taken your innocence, and I must now pay the forfeit for my scandalous lack of self-control."

"Pay the forfeit," she repeated. "You make it sound as if wedding me would be a chore."

"Not a chore," he denied, "but it would not be my choice. You would not be my choice."

The arrow of heat turned into a dart of hurt, lodging itself in her heart. "You are doing a dreadful job of attempting to persuade me to marry you, Lord Hertford."

"It would please me if you called me Cam," he said, reaching for her hand, which was clenching a fist in the counterpane, once more. "And I am being honest with you. Utterly, completely honest. I owe you that much. Christ, I owe you a lot more than that, but I will begin here: I desire you. Prior to arriving here in Oxfordshire, prior to having met you, I would never have wanted you as my countess because of the scandal darkening your name."

She stiffened. "My lord—"

"Allow me to finish, if you please," he interrupted. "Honesty, Eugie. The Prince of Proper could not bear to accept a wife whose reputation was not as pristine as his. But then I saw you in the ballroom, and you were wearing that red gown, and your lips matched, and you spoke to me with such assurance. When we danced, something happened.

"From the beginning, I have wanted you in a way that consternates and perplexes me. You are beautiful, and you are wealthy, but you are all wrong for me. Your brother is a tradesman. Your reputation is tarnished. And yet, I can think of nothing but you. When I see you, I want to kiss you. When I am alone with you, I lose my ability to resist temptation."

Somehow, in the course of his unexpected soliloquy, the tension had ebbed from her fingers. She had ceased grasping the bed linens. Instead, her hand had relaxed, turning so her palm faced upward, and their fingers had laced together once more.

His confession was strangely endearing.

And she could understand the sentiment behind it, for she

felt the same way. Whenever she was in his presence, all she wanted to do was kiss him again. To touch him. The strength of his shoulders, the muscles of his arms, to lay her lips upon him everywhere she could.

Where their hands met, a tingling awareness began and radiated up her arm, pooling ultimately between her thighs. Her body had not forgotten his.

"I do not want to be your regret, Eugie," he continued. "But neither can I allow my sins to go unanswered for. I have dishonored you, and I must make it right."

"No one knows," she said. "Our secret is safe."

"*I* know," he said sternly. "And you know."

She tried, quite furiously, to think of the cottage. The roses. The elusive dream of freedom. "I have a plan, Lord Hertford. I will buy my freedom with my fortune."

"Or, you could buy mine," he suggested simply.

"Yours," she repeated.

"Mine. If you do not wed me, I may have to find another bride with an immense dowry, and I will have to reveal to her that I once despoiled an innocent. She will resent me to her dying day, and our marriage will be cold and chaste, and I will never sire an heir." He squeezed her fingers. "And you will be all alone in your cottage with no one to enjoy the roses but you. What color would they be?"

Once again, his wandering mind had her flummoxed. "The roses?"

"Yes."

"White," she said, for she had already given some thought to her fancy. "There is something about the absence of color which makes them so beautiful."

"Grow them at Lyndhurst House." His thumb was rubbing lazy circles upon her inner wrist now, weakening her resolve. "White ones and red ones too, to match your lips."

"What is Lyndhurst House?" she asked, though she could surmise well enough.

"My country seat in Lincolnshire." His thumb traveled higher, that simple caress enough to make her weak all over again. "My father stripped it of everything of value, squandering all he could on vice. We can rebuild it together. Think of it this way, Eugie. It shall be an even bargain between us. You can save me from ruin, and I shall save you as well."

An even bargain.

Why, oh why, had he asked her about the roses? She was sure she could have denied him if he had overlooked that infinitesimal detail. And if he was not crowding her with his large, masculine body, his warmth, his handsome face, that mouth, his scent…

"I shall consider your proposal, Lord Hertford," she allowed before she could think better of it.

But it could not be helped, not when he was touching her as he was, and gazing upon her in such a manner. He was turning her insides to liquid.

"Cam," he corrected softly. "If you are to be my wife, you may as well grow accustomed to my given name."

"I did not say I would marry you," she reminded him sharply, before thinking better of it and lowering her voice back to a whisper. "I said I would *consider* the prospect. Now please do go before you are caught here, and the rumors that dreadful man spread about me are the least of our worries."

He released her hand, leaving her feeling bereft. "If anyone deserves a blackened eye, it is Cunningham," he said grimly. "And I am of half a mind to give him one myself."

His words warmed her. But she chased the warmth. "Go now, my lord."

"Very well." At last, he stood.

And this new distance between them, too, she felt like a

loss. With great effort, she remained where she was, watching as he delivered an elegant bow, as though they faced each other in the formality of the drawing room.

"Sleep well, Eugie."

"Good evening, Lord Hertford," she whispered back.

"Cam," he corrected in hushed tones. "Or husband, if you prefer."

She bit her lip at his persistence. "Go away, my lord."

And, taking his brace of candles with him, he disappeared back into the night.

But slumber did not follow in his wake. All she could think was she did not dare trust him. And she did not dare accept his proposal. She would be far better served to find her cottage and hide herself there.

When she finally did fall asleep, she dreamt of roses and Cam.

Chapter Ten

*S*LEIGH RIDES WERE in order for the day, because an early snow had blanketed the countryside. The powdery whiteness clung lovingly to barren branches, coating the undulating hills and fields. As always, the newly fallen snow filled Cam with a sense of awe. An appreciation for the peacefulness of nature, the beauty of the world around him.

But that appreciation paled in comparison to the lady at his side.

Miss Eugie Winter was seated alongside him, blankets covering her lap, warm bricks at her feet. Nearly all of her was hidden, in fact. Her gloved hands were inside a fur muff, and a pelisse hid her pleasing feminine shape from him. Her lovely face stood out against the backdrop of snow, a dashing hat keeping her silken brunette locks from his gaze. Her ribbons, he noted, were firmly tied this time.

The chilled air had brought a lush pink to her cheeks, and her lips, too, were kissed with cold.

God, he could not stop stealing looks at her.

He was like a lad, fawning over the first female to pay him any heed. What he felt for her was strange. He had never before experienced anything its equal. He wanted her kisses. All of them. He wanted her smiles, to be their source. He wanted to be her reason to laugh. He wanted to touch her, to feel her beneath him. The combination of desire and something deeper was foreign.

Frightening.

"You are friends with Viscount Aylesford," she said at last, breaking the silence between them.

The topic was not one he would have preferred. His hands tightened on the reins as he drove them over a gently swelling hill, leaving Abingdon House and their fellow house guests out of sight behind them.

"I am," he agreed, slanting another look in her direction. "Why do you ask?"

"He is attempting to convince my sister to engage in a feigned betrothal with him," Eugie said. "I do not trust his motives."

The words he had heard her say to her sister in the library that day returned to him, words she had spoken about Cam himself.

He is a fortune hunter like all the rest, of course.

She was jaded, Miss Eugie Winter. And something—or rather someone—had made her that way. He gripped the reigns tighter and clenched his jaw as the need to plant Cunningham a facer rose within him once again.

"I suspect you do not trust anyone's motives," he observed. "Including mine."

Another glance in her direction revealed her lush lips had tightened, her chin tipping upward in defiance. "Trust must be earned, not freely given."

"Fair enough, Eugie."

"I never gave you leave to call me Eugie," she pointed out.

"Do you not think us beyond formality?" He cast another look in her direction. Their gazes clashed, and something gripped him, deep within.

Something unfathomable.

In her eyes, he could see the heat of awareness, the flare of remembrance. But then her gaze grew shuttered once more. "I think I have been inexcusably foolish where you are concerned, my lord."

Yes, she had. And, likewise, so had he.

But her response filled him with disappointment just the same. He cleared his throat and returned his attention to the vista ahead of them. The sleigh drew softly, slowly over the snow. He was timing their outing with care. They could not be gone for too long. Just a few minutes more before he needed to turn around and return them to Abingdon House.

For all that he had gone beyond the bounds of propriety with her, committing the ultimate sin without benefit of matrimony, he was determined to keep her reputation as scandal-free moving forward as possible.

It would not do to encourage gossip to flourish. Thankfully, given the tight space of the open sleigh, the coldness of the air, and the festive nature of the house party, they had some latitude.

Just enough, he hoped.

"We have both been foolish," he allowed then, "but I am attempting to set matters right."

"By marrying me and gaining my fortune," she said cynically. "And absolving your debt."

"By marrying you so I can have you in my bed." Just the thought sent a rush of heat to his loins. "In my arms. So I can kiss you whenever I wish."

Silence descended between them once more, and he feared he had gone too far, that he had pushed too hard. Had he shocked her? He had not meant to be so forthright, but Eugie Winter did something to him. She had changed him.

"What a wicked thing for the Prince of Proper to say," she murmured at last.

But she did not sound shocked.

Rather, she sounded intrigued.

"I suppose it is better to be wicked than to be a pompous bore," he could not resist teasing.

A surprised burst of laughter left her for just a moment until she squelched it. "I was dreadfully rude to you at the welcome ball, was I not?"

Damn him, but the sound of her laughter curled around his heart, squeezing it tight. "We were rude to each other, as I recall."

The time had come to turn the sled and begin making their way back to Abingdon House, and he already dreaded the hours they would spend apart. What was it about her that so bewitched him? That made him weak in a way no other woman before her ever had?

"I am sorry for insulting you," she said quietly as he steered them in the direction from which they had come. "After Baron Cunningham spread such vicious gossip about me, I find myself distrusting everyone."

Her candor pleased him, but the mention of Cunningham once more filled him with unanswered anger. Something had to be done about a blackguard who would stoop so low. Along with it, came guilt. For he had believed the gossip.

"And I am sorry for judging you before I knew you," he returned.

He looked over just in time to catch her sending a small smile his way. "Thank you, Cam."

It was not much, but as the sun glinted off the snow around them and the horses plodded back home, her use of his given name again at last rather felt like a victory.

THE PARLOR GAME of the evening was snapdragon, but Eugie

was not in the mood to attempt to rescue a raisin from a brandy-soaked flame and risk catching the sleeve of her gown on fire in the process. Instead, she had wandered to the library, where pine boughs had been liberally hung in preparation for Christmas Day. A fire crackled merrily in the massive hearth, and braces of candles and chandeliers brightened the room with a warm glow.

It was all quite cozy and festive. But the beauty of it was lost upon her, for she was too caught up in her own musings. For several days now, Cam had been courting her. There was no other word to describe it. He was charming her.

Wooing her.

And her heart was having a difficult time resisting him.

As was the rest of her.

"I thought I may find you here."

The deep timbre of his voice was unmistakable, setting off a shiver of awareness she could not fight. Eugie turned to find him striding toward her, unfairly handsome in his evening wear. He had been the perfect gentleman ever since the night he had trespassed in her bedchamber.

The Prince of Proper in truth, always impeccable, always above reproach. She missed his kiss. Part of her—perhaps *all* of her, even—liked him wicked.

"You followed me," she accused without heat.

For in truth, something inside her came to life at the sight of him. After little time alone over the last few days, the chance to be with just him appealed.

"I did." The grin he sent her was unrepentant. Boyish, almost. He stopped, near enough to touch. "But not before securing a handful of raisins at the expense of my fingers."

"Did you burn yourself?" Without thought, she reached for his gloveless hands, turning them over for her inspection.

Just as quickly, he flipped her hands over, clasping them

in his warm grip. "It stung, but I shall live."

His scent washed over her, and her body's response was instant. She was falling into his eyes. And she was oh-so aware of everything—the space separating their mouths, the crackling of the fire in the distance, the blowing of the wind beyond the walls of Abingdon House, the heat rolling off his big body.

"Do you realize where you are standing, Eugie?" he asked softly.

Unwisely near to him, but she could not bear to take a step away. Could not bear to break the connection of their hands or gazes.

"Right here," she said.

"Look up," he told her, his sensual lips curving into a smile so tender, she felt it in her core.

There was such promise there, so much delicious intent.

For a moment, she could do nothing other than stare at him, drinking in the sight of him in the candlelight, this man with whom she had shared such shocking intimacies. This man who felt so familiar and right.

But then she forced herself to look up at last, and when she did, it was to find a sprig of mistletoe hanging overhead, suspended from the beam supporting the second floor of the library. Hunger flared to life. Desire began as a throb between her thighs and turned into a great, pulsing need that threatened to consume her.

She glanced back to find him watching her in a manner that stole her breath.

"Oh," was all she could think of saying.

Not even a coherent sentence.

Because she felt unaccountably shy in this moment. It was different. Their other kisses had been sudden and reckless, or hidden in darkness. They had been covert and secret. They had not been in the well-lit library where anyone could come upon them at any moment. They had not been after he had declared his intention to marry her.

"I am obliged to steal a kiss," he said.

"And then my dowry," she quipped, forcing herself to recall all the reasons why he was wrong for her. Why this was wrong.

Why she must not allow a kiss with him to cloud her judgment.

"I am the best kind of fortune hunter you can find, Eugie Winter," he told her, drawing her nearer by their linked hands. "An honest one."

Yes, he had been truthful with her, had he not?

He had been candid about his debts, his scoundrel father. He had promised her a mutually beneficial solution to their problems instead. She had no idea why that seemed so appealing to her.

Cottage, she reminded herself. *Think of the cottage. The roses.*

"There is no good kind of fortune hunter," she forced herself to say.

But she did not break their entwined hands. Nor did she step away.

"Mayhap you might think of me as a man instead," he suggested, his gaze dipping to her lips. "A man who wants you very much. A man who wishes to be your husband. A man who is going to kiss you."

And then, his mouth was on hers.

Chapter Eleven

I T WAS ALL the fault of the mistletoe.

That, and Eugie's berry-red lips, beckoning him. He missed them beneath his, the plush suppleness of them, so pliant and sweet. Better than dessert. He was kissing her now, consuming her really, like the delicacy she was. She tasted of punch and Christmas and delicious woman, and he could not get enough.

He could never get enough.

Why had he allowed so many days to lapse between the last time he had owned her soft mouth and now? He did not know, but the instant his tongue swept past the seam of her lips, he vowed to make up for the lost time. The same fervor that overcame him whenever he touched her returned, stronger than ever.

Taking his breath.

Robbing his ability to think.

He released their entwined fingers so he could touch her as he longed. Everywhere. His hands traveled up her waist, higher still, over her thudding heart, to the pulse pounding on the soft column of her throat, burying in her nape. Her hair was silken.

Everything about her was rich and lustrous, so vibrant. Her fragrance of blossoming summer garden enveloped him. All his good intentions vanished, along with his need to maintain propriety. Because she was in his arms where she belonged, and her tongue was playing against his, the bounty of her breasts crushed into his chest.

And *Christ*, but he could feel the hardness of her nipples prodding him like twin diamonds through all their combined layers. He could not resist finding them and tweaking the buds, rolling them between his thumb and forefinger until he earned a moan from deep in her throat. Husky and mellifluous, that sound made him want more.

He sucked on her lower lip, then nipped it with his teeth, overwhelmed by the voracious need to claim her. And then he licked away the sting before kissing her deeper, then finding his way down her neck to her ear. He nuzzled the hollow there, pleased to discover how sensitive she was when he used his tongue to advantage. A few well-placed licks, and her hands were on his shoulders, her nails digging into his muscles like a kitten's claws.

Yes, he wanted her ferocious. He wanted her as desperate as he was. Now that he had begun, he could not stop. He had intended to take one kiss from her beneath the mistletoe ball. He ought to have known better. Ought to have understood he could never stop at just one kiss when it came to Eugie Winter.

He was desperate to be inside her again, his cock rigid and aching, as he recalled the heat and grip of her, the feeling of sliding home. He bit the fleshy lobe of her ear, then kissed the shell, rocking into her softness with his hardness. Letting her feel how much he wanted her. And he could tell the moment she understood, for she emitted a gasp, and then moved nearer to him, until every part of their bodies was flush, from head to toe.

"Marry me," he whispered into her ear.

He could not take her again until they were wed, he told

himself. Though he had been making every effort to earn her trust and win her hand, she had yet to let down her walls. But now, he could almost feel something inside her shifting. Could feel the same response in himself.

He was changing.

She had changed him.

And he welcomed that, just as he welcomed her. Because he wanted roses in his gardens and Eugie in his bed. He wanted the woman in the red dress who had looked upon him with such scorn when they had met. He wanted the lady who loved gardens and libraries in equal measure. The lady who was wicked. The lady whose reputation was altogether wrong.

He had always wanted her, from that first night on, although he had known he should not. And he wanted her now, more than ever. More with each kiss. Each breath.

But she had not answered him. He raised his head and stared down into her upturned face, into those warm, brown eyes with their impossibly thick lashes. Into the face of the woman he wanted to make his countess.

The woman he wanted to spend every night with for the rest of his life.

The woman he loved.

"Eugie," he rasped, needing to fill the silence that had descended between them with something. Needing to chase away the realization he was not yet ready to accept.

Love? Could it be?

"I..." Her words trailed off, and she frowned, looking away from him. "I am not ready to accept such a fate yet."

Such a fate.

He stiffened, inwardly grasping the vexation her words inspired in him with both hands. "The notion of becoming my countess still displeases you?"

She swallowed. "I scarcely know you."

"What do you wish to know of me?" he asked, frustration rising, mingling with the desire, warring for supremacy.

"Everything," she said, her eyes wide. "I need more time, Cam. The notion of binding myself to you, knowing you are in need of my dowry…it frightens me."

He was going to beat Cunningham to a pulp when he returned to London. And then he was going to personally launch a campaign to restore Eugie's reputation. Not because she was his wife—as long as he could convince her to wed him, of course—but because she deserved to shine. She deserved to hold her head high and sail through society like the goddess she was. He would silence the whispers, *by God*.

"Look at me, Eugie," he said softly, cupping her face in his hands. "You can trust me. Believe what you will of me, but I promise you I am a man of my word. I may need your dowry to save my estates from ruin, but I, too, have something to offer you in return."

"I do not need a title to be happy," Eugie told him softly.

He knew she was being utterly truthful. But he had come to understand her well enough to know being a countess was not enough lure to sway her. There was something else, he felt certain, which was.

He had witnessed, firsthand, the closeness of the Winter family. Devereaux Winter loved his sisters with a ferocity he had not often seen. Cam had found much to admire in the man during his stay at Abingdon Hall.

And he knew Eugie cared for her brother and her sisters with a love that was rare and generous and altruistic. Another rarity in his experience.

"What of your family, Eugie?" he pressed. "Do you think your family would be happy to see you hide yourself in shame in the country, living your life alone in some godforsaken cottage? I have seen how much you all love each other, and I cannot believe they would accept such a lonely fate for you, even should you want it for yourself."

She stared up at him, and he wished he could hear her thoughts.

"Who says my cottage shall be godforsaken?" she asked at last, a small smile upon her kiss-swollen lips. "I will have roses there, after all. Perhaps a small library of my own. And no one will ever whisper about me again."

It was like her to jest. He was beginning to know her. To understand her. And he wanted the chance to continue. He was not willing to give her up. He was determined.

"You will have roses wherever you live when you are my countess," he promised. "And you may replace all the books in the library with volumes of your choosing. If anyone whispers about you, they will have me to answer to. Most importantly, you will never need to hide. You will hold your head high."

Her countenance turned sad. "I already hold my head high. I do not need a champion, Cam."

He begged to differ, but he would not press the matter. "Think of your sisters, Eugie. If we wed, it will go a long way toward enabling them to secure good matches as well. Your brother is hungry for the respectability marrying into the nobility will bring him and his family. I can give you that."

"Cam."

"White roses, Eugie. Wherever you wish," he prodded, using her words against her.

"Cam," she said again, but her voice had softened, along with her expression. She looked almost tender. "I can already have white roses wherever I wish."

Of course she could. She was a Winter, and the Winter family was one of the wealthiest in all England.

He ran his thumb over the proud line of her cheek. "But you cannot have my kisses whenever you wish."

Her eyes darkened. She ran her tongue over her bottom lip, and he had to suppress a groan at the sight.

"I already have them whenever I wish," she countered.

"I will not follow you to your cottage," he said, and then he could not resist lowering his lips to her forehead. "I will not do this." He kissed the tip of her nose. "Or this." Then her cheek. "Nor this." He settled upon her lips at last. "Definitely not this."

And then he was kissing her again, kissing her with all the passion once more flaring to life inside him. Because he could not stop. Did not dare stop. He would persuade her by any means he had, and if she would not listen to reason, perhaps she would listen to the fire burning between them.

EUGIE COULD NOT resist that mouth.

His mouth.

Cam's.

Cam. Oh heavens, he knew how to kiss. Or perhaps he just knew how to kiss her. Or his lips were made to fit hers perfectly. He was trying his best to convince her to marry him, and she knew it. She could not be certain if it was her dowry he wanted most or the erasure of the guilt he must carry around with him for taking her virtue.

And not only did he know how to kiss, but he also knew how to persuade. Knew when to persuade with his lips and tongue instead of his words.

She kissed him back, of course she did. And her hands were in his hair now, cradling his skull, fingers tunneling through the short, thick locks that were softer than they looked. And she was breathing him in, and his tongue was in her mouth, one of his hands settled on her hip, the other on the small of her back, guiding her into the prominent ridge of his manhood.

He wanted her.

And to her shame, the knowledge sent an answering throb to her core. She was wet for him. Aching for him. Deep within her, she longed for the unparalleled sensation of her body joined with his.

Because she wanted him, too.

She should not. She did not dare accept his suit. There was still so much she needed to learn about him. So many questions. But with his mouth devouring hers, she could not think of a single query to pose. Nor could she recall one opposition to becoming his countess.

The Countess of Hertford.

How strange, how silly to imagine herself owning such an appellation. A quivery sensation slid through her. A lightness mingled with heaviness, as though she were flitting outside her body and yet trapped within it, all at once.

She had never aspired to become a nobleman's wife.

That was a dream of her brother's, a misguided notion he maintained that they would all be happy if they could free themselves of the ties which bound them inextricably to their sordid past. Their father had been a cruel man. A ruthless man. A tyrant. And the basis for their wealth had been accumulated in all the wrong manners. Dev tried to make up for it now. They all did.

But the scars of the past lingered. Every now and then, the skin drew taught. The wounds opened.

Dev thought marrying into the quality would change things for them all.

She was not as certain it could, but when the Earl of Hertford's tongue was in her mouth, she was not certain of anything. Even her own name.

"Cam," she whispered against his lips, his name, a plea.

"Tell me yes," he murmured back, and then he was sucking on her lower lip once more, licking into her mouth. His hands were roving over her body in a welcomed claiming. He found her breasts with one; another cupped her rump, angling her body to his so he could press his length into the heart of her.

She wanted to tell him *yes*.

Mayhap she should.

But the word would not arrive on her lips. Perhaps because she was so consumed in him. By him. With him. He sucked her tongue into his mouth, and an answering burst of need fired to life deep inside her. The act was so sinful, so carnal, and she had never experienced anything like it.

The Prince of Proper had untold wickedness. And she liked that, too.

In truth, she liked *him*. She liked the wildness in him that had made him kiss her in the darkened hall that night. The way he had kissed her all the way across his bedchamber. The passion that had led them to fall together in his bed. She liked the tender way he touched and held her, the way he kissed her. She liked the way he looked at her, from across a chamber. As if she were the only woman he saw.

He made her feel that way, too. As if she alone stole his attention. As if she alone was the one he wanted, the one he needed above all others, and not just for her dowry but for her, on an elemental level. For herself as a woman. No man had ever made her feel thus. Not even Cunningham, though he had put on a grand show of affections in the beginning, all the better to manipulate her.

The reminder of her past and what it had cost her should have hit her with a renewed surge of bitterness. But instead, she felt transformed in Cam's arms. For the first time, she felt as if she were clipping the weights of what had happened in the past.

She was lighter. Freer.

And she grew bolder. Braver. Her teeth found his lip and bit, drawing on him as he had done to her. Her reward was a groan, emerging from deep within his broad chest. And then, his hands clamped on her waist. He lifted her into his arms. She clung to him.

"Say you will be my wife," he said again, as he settled her upon a settee with great care.

He handled her as if she were fashioned of finest china. As if she were something breakable. Something precious. And it made her want to weep and kiss him all at once. Instead, she remained where he had placed her, sitting on the edge of the settee, the skirts of her gown billowing around her.

Cam towered over her until he sank to his knees on the thick carpets, placing his hands upon her knees. "Eugie, please."

Still, she could not form the word. "I am not ready, Cam."

Her heart had fooled her once before. It could fool her again.

"Have you forgotten you could be carrying my babe?" he demanded, his expression turning hard.

As hard as stone.

It seemed as if she could cut her fingers on his cheek bones or the rigidity of his jaw.

"I am not," she denied, though she had no reason to suggest she wasn't. She understood that she would not be free of worry until she had her courses, and those had yet to arrive.

"You cannot be certain," he countered.

And he was not wrong in that, but she would never admit it.

117

"Even if I am, I will take care of myself," she countered. "The babe will want for nothing. You need not fret over that. I've money aplenty to see him raised properly."

For it was true. Dev had control of her portion of the Winter fortune, but she was sure she could convince him to relinquish it to her, to allow her to set herself up in a cottage somewhere. Anywhere she wished. She could do that. She was strong.

His grasp on her knees tightened. "The hell you will raise my child on your own. Eugie, you must see reason. I know you suffered because of Cunningham, and I promise you, I will enact my own vengeance upon him when the time comes, but I am not him. I want to marry you, and not just for your fortune, but for you."

For you.

She had not expected those two, simple words to affect her as much as they did.

But they did.

She did not want to believe them. It hardly seemed possible a man could want her for herself. Indeed, it hardly seemed possible *Cam* could want her for herself. She still did not dare trust him. Even after all they had shared.

Her heart was such a fool.

She was weak, so very weak, for him.

"You need my dowry," she countered, finding her tongue at last.

"I need *you*," he returned, and the intensity of his gaze was undeniable.

"The mistletoe is over there," she said weakly, gesturing to the part of the library they had abandoned.

"To the devil with the mistletoe." He rose on his knees, and then his mouth was on hers once more.

Her arms wrapped around his neck, and she drew herself

nearer to him. Wanting more. Wanting him so much she did not hear the library door click open or realize they were no longer alone until the shocked feminine gasp echoing through the massive chamber intruded upon her idyll.

She broke free of Cam, jerking her mouth from his too late.

The Duchess of Revelstoke stood on the threshold of the library, along with her son Viscount Aylesford, and another dowager who was a notorious gossip, the Marchioness of Heath.

"Hertford, is that you?" demanded the duchess, her tone horrified and strident.

Cutting through the silence like a slap.

"Damnation," Cam muttered.

She stared down at him, her heart sinking like a leaden weight in her chest as the truth hit her with such force she almost cried out.

He had planned this farce.

And she would never, ever forgive him for it.

Chapter Twelve

"*I* OUGHT TO call you out for this."

Devereaux Winter's voice seethed with fury, and Cam did not blame him one whit. He was seated opposite Mr. Winter in the expansive study of Abingdon House, feeling as if he were facing his executioner.

"I would call me out as well," he acknowledged into the biting silence. "I cannot convey how deeply sorry I am for causing the threat of more scandal for Eugie."

"Eugie, is it?" Winter scrubbed a hand over his jaw. "You have daring, Hertford."

What he had was stupidity and an aching cock.

But Cam wasn't about to venture as much aloud. Because he was a fool, but he was not mad. And the prospect of matching Devereaux Winter in a bout of fisticuffs, swords, or pistols was not exactly heartening.

"Miss Winter," he corrected himself. "Pray excuse my familiarity, Mr. Winter. I harbor a great deal of affection for your sister, though my unacceptable actions today did not demonstrate that."

"Your actions were unacceptable, you say." Winter's voice was bitter, his lip curled in a sneer. "I would call them careless, thoughtless, selfish, and idiotic, more like."

Cam swallowed. It went against the grain to allow himself to be maligned, especially by a man who was not a peer of the realm, but Devereaux Winter was a breed of his own, and Cam had compromised the man's sister.

Far more thoroughly than he supposed.

And to Cam's everlasting shame.

"I deserve every insult you choose to hurl my way," he conceded. "And more. Believe me when I say harming Miss Winter's reputation is the last thing I ever wanted to do."

"Which is why you were alone with her in the library, pawing at her as if she were a Covent Garden lightskirt," Winter said grimly.

His ears went hot, and another arrow of shame sank into his gut, chasing away the lingering hunger he felt for Eugie. At least for the moment. Until he thought of her again. Remembered the sweetness of her kiss or the lush eroticism of her scent.

"I deeply regret the nature of my actions earlier toward Miss Winter," he forced himself to say. "I will be more than happy to do anything in my power to rectify the damage which has been done."

Winter continued to glower at him. "What do you suggest? Marrying her and helping yourself to her fortune, I suppose."

Yes, but not like that.

Marrying her because he had bedded her. Because she could be carrying his child. Because he had been trailing after her this entire blasted house party like a puppy following his master.

Most importantly of all, because he loved her.

He cleared his throat. "Mr. Winter, I have tender feelings for Miss Winter."

"Tender feelings." Winter watched him with the predatory stare of a hunter, looking for weakness, taking his aim.

"Yes." He paused, for he had never before asked to marry

a woman. And he had certainly never fallen in love with one, nor revealed his emotions to the brother of the lady in question. It was a deuced awkward affair.

"Naturally, your tender feelings have nothing to do with her dowry or the wealth she stands to receive upon her nuptials," Winter said bitterly.

"It does not." Cam searched for the proper words and found nothing. "I am drowning in my father's debts, it is true. I have been honest with Miss Winter concerning my circumstances. Circumstances which, I trust, were also instrumental in my invitation to this house party."

Winter raised a brow. "What are you suggesting, Hertford?"

"That it is no secret you are looking to secure titles for your sisters," he said. "I find it odd indeed you should look down your nose at me for the same reasons you extended me your hospitality. I am in need of a wealthy wife, your sisters are on the marriage mart, and you are looking to acquire the respectability all the money in the world cannot buy."

Mr. Winter drummed his fingers on the polished surface of the desk. "As I said, you have daring, Hertford."

"I speak honestly," he said, taking a deep breath before proceeding. "Which is why I must tell you the indiscretion in the library is not the first occasion during which I compromised Miss Winter."

He would spare himself and Eugie both the embarrassment of revealing all to her brother, but he would not pretend to be innocent. If he was going to win Eugie as his wife, he owed it to the both of them to secure her hand in the right fashion. With honesty and integrity.

Or whatever shreds of those he still possessed.

"I beg your pardon," Winter said then, with deceptive calm.

Deceptive because whilst his voice was even and cool, his visage had darkened, taking on a rigid, thunderous mien. He looked as if, at any moment, he would explode in a fit of violent rage.

"I have compromised Miss Winter before today," he elaborated.

"Was this a plan, then?" Winter asked, and again his voice was quiet.

He was the snake poised to strike.

"There was no plan," he defended himself. "The truth of the matter is, I was privy to the gossip surrounding Miss Winter when I met her. I had deemed her unsuitable."

Winter's fist slammed down on the desk with such abrupt force, Cam nearly jumped. "How dare you?"

"But I fell in love with her," he confessed, meeting Winter's gaze, unflinching. "I am not certain when it happened or how. All I do know is that I cannot live without her as my wife, and not because of her fortune, but because of the lady herself. She turned any notions I had of her upon their head, and she made me realize a great deal about myself in the process."

"You expect me to believe you are in love with my sister." Winter stared at him now as if he were an escaped Bedlamite.

"I do not expect or require you to believe anything," Cam said calmly. "Your belief or lack thereof will not make it any less true. I love Miss Winter, and it would be my greatest honor to make her my countess."

"You truly love her?" Winter pressed.

"I do." Cam did not hesitate in his response. Loving Eugie felt inevitable. It felt right. He wanted her in his life, at his side, in his bed. He wanted her roses in his garden, her books in his library, her hair fanned over his pillow every night, her lips on his.

"If you love her," Winter began, watching him carefully now, "then you will marry her without her fortune."

"Yes." Once again, he did not waver. "Even if I must sell off the estates and everything remaining my bastard of a sire did not already take, I will marry her. Supposing she will deign to have me, of course."

She had not agreed to wed him.

And after the stricken expression on her face earlier, he was not certain she would. But he was determined to try. He had to try, because the notion of marrying anyone else was impossible. It was Eugie Winter or no one at all.

"Then I am afraid that is what you must do," Winter said. "I will grant my approval of a match between you and my sister, Hertford, but by the conditions of my father's will, the fortunes of my sisters remain at my disposal until the births of their first children, or as I see fit. You will not see a shilling of her dowry upon your marriage to her."

It was a blow he had not anticipated, to be sure, but Cam would weather it. He would make a plan. He had already begun the task of deciding which properties must go first. He would merely continue.

"I accept your conditions, sir," he said.

"Oh, but I have one more," Winter added, flashing him a grim smile. "My sister must agree to the match as well."

"She will," he vowed with a confidence that was perhaps fatuous.

But he had to believe he could win Eugie's heart and her hand both. Because if he could not, he would be lost.

EUGIE WAS SHEPHERDED to one of the smaller salons of Abingdon House—a yellow one dotted with dozens of portraits—by her sister-in-law, Lady Emilia. In the wake of her ignominy, a strange tumult of sensations buffeted her.

Disappointment.

Hurt.

Anger.

Self-loathing.

"Sit, dearest," Lady Emilia ordered her.

Though her tone was gentle, it was firm. Eugie obeyed, settling herself upon a chair. "I am sorry I have ruined your marvelous party," she apologized at once before her sister-in-law had had the chance to properly seat herself.

Emilia frowned at her as she descended gracefully upon a gilded settee. "I do not care about the party, Eugie. I care about you."

Eugie fretted with the skirt of her gown, plucking at it as if it were an instrument string. "I am sorry for ruining myself."

Her sister-in-law sighed. "You are not ruined. Yet. Whether or not you truly are depends upon what you choose to do next."

"I will not marry him," she denied swiftly. "I am sorry, my lady, but I cannot bear it."

"Oh, Eugie." Emilia sighed, her countenance softening. "Lord Hertford is the one after all, is he not?"

Eugie's cheeks flushed, for there was no need for her sister-in-law to elaborate. Cam had always been the one. He was the *only* one. But he had betrayed her, and she could not trust him. "I have kissed him before today," she admitted.

"You promised me you would not be so reckless," Emilia chided.

Yes, she had, to her everlasting shame. But she was no match for the Earl of Hertford's mouth or his knowing hands. How quickly she had fallen beneath his thrall. How easily he had manipulated her, wooed her. Tricked her into believing, for a desperate moment, everything he had told her was real.

That he wanted to marry her not because of her fortune, but because he cared for her. Because he wanted her. How wrong she had been.

"I am sorry," she said, lowering her gaze to her lap, where her fingers were clenching her skirts so tightly, her knuckles had gone white. "I betrayed your trust, and I have brought shame upon you and my sisters. You were so good to do your utmost to restore my reputation after the lies Cunningham spread. I did not deserve your kindness before, and I do not deserve it now."

"Nonsense," Emilia said firmly. "You have a good heart, Eugie Winter, and you deserve every kindness. You also deserve happiness. You deserve to claim your place in society. You can do that now, and you will spare yourself and your sisters both."

"By marrying him," Eugie surmised. "But I cannot do that, Emilia. He arranged for us to be seen. I know he did—only think of it, we were interrupted by his friend and his friend's mother and her bosom bow. He had been asking me to marry him for days, and I had told him I would not."

"Why did you refuse him?" her sister-in-law asked.

"Because I do not dare trust him, for fear he will break my heart," she admitted, biting her lip to stave off a rush of humiliating tears she had no wish to indulge.

Yes, there it was. The bitter, awful truth. She had fallen in love with the Earl of Hertford. Cam. The man who kissed her so sweetly, who had made love to her with such tenderness. The man she had been drawn to from the moment they had danced together at the welcome ball.

The man she could not shake.

She loved him. But she was terrified he did not love her in

return. Fearful he only wanted her fortune, which he freely admitted he needed to save himself from ruin.

"Why would he break your heart?" Emilia's shrewd voice cut through her wild thoughts.

"I have fallen in love with him," she whispered. "But I have already been deceived and hurt badly by another. I did not love the baron, and I know that now. But if I were to discover Cam only wanted to marry me to avail himself of my fortune, I… I do not think I could bear it."

"Eugie," her sister-in-law pressed softly. "I understand all too well how you feel. Love is terrifying. It is like a massive beast, holding us in its grasp, with the power to keep us safe or crush us in equal measure. When I fell in love with your brother, I was fearful too. I ran from him, because running was easier than facing the way I felt."

The love her brother and his wife shared was undeniable. The way they looked at each other was enough to warm her heart and to make her yearn for that same powerful connection. But Cam had never spoken one word of love to her. Nor did she expect him to, especially after the farce he had arranged earlier.

"It is different for you and Dev," she insisted. "You are both desperately in love with each other.

"I believe you and the earl are in love with each other too," Emilia said then. "I selected the guests for this house party with great care, doing my best to find gentlemen I believed could make good matches with you. Lord Hertford's reputation, aside from today's indiscretion, is impeccable. You could do no better. I also suspect he is in love with you, my dear. Otherwise, he would never behave in such a reckless fashion."

"He would if he wanted my share of the Winter wealth," she argued, mulish.

SCARLETT SCOTT

"If that were true, he could have compromised you immediately. He could have arranged for such a tableau when he first kissed you," her sister-in-law returned. "He could have left you without a choice well before now."

As Emilia's words took root in her mind, some of the anger she had been harboring toward Cam abated. He had been giving her a choice, had he not? Emilia was right. He could have forced her hand when he had first kissed her. Or later, when he had made love to her. He could have gone to Dev and revealed everything, leaving her with one option to save herself.

He had never hidden the truth about his debts. Indeed, he had always been open and honest about them. And whilst he had been asking her to marry him at every step of the way, he had always accepted her denial.

What if he had not arranged for them to be discovered earlier at all? What if he had been every bit as shocked at the interruption as she had been? What if she had been wrong about him, just as he had once been wrong about her?

"You have much to think about," Emilia added gently. "This is not a matter of the next day or the next week. This is a matter of the rest of your life. I have spoken with your brother, and he is adamant that the choice must be yours and yours alone. He will not pressure you to accept Hertford's offer of marriage, and neither shall I."

"His offer of marriage?" she repeated. "Has he... He has gone to Dev, then?"

Lady Emilia nodded. "Of course he has. Your brother was furious when he heard the news. An interview was in order. You must have expected as much."

She supposed she had, but somehow not as quickly as it had occurred. In the aftermath of her recklessness, she had been bustled from the chamber, separated from Cam as if she were kindling and he the flame and everyone feared they would burst into a raging fire at any second.

"I have never been truly ruined before," she said at last, attempting levity. "Merely rumored to have been. I was not certain how such matters work."

"Lord Hertford wishes an audience with you now, and Dev and I are willing to allow it," Emilia surprised her by saying. "The door will remain ajar, and we will be near enough that if either one of you so much as coughs, we shall hear it. But this matter must be settled, and it must be done today. Tarrying much longer will only bring scandal down upon the both of you. Aylesford will not speak, and he assures me his mother shall not either, but the Marchioness of Heath will not be so generous."

Eugie swallowed. Cam wanted to speak with her. Now.

She was not sure she was ready to face him yet. Her armor was not in place. And she was confused. So terribly confused. "I do not know what to do," she confessed to her sister-in-law.

"Follow your heart," Emilia told her. "Trust it to make the right choice."

Chapter Thirteen

"IFTEEN MINUTES," DEVEREAUX Winter breathed down his neck.

Thankfully, the man's wife was a far gentler creature. Cam was already nervous enough at the notion of convincing Eugie to agree to marry him with a time limit and an audience awaiting her decision.

Lady Emilia smiled at him reassuringly. "We will be just down the hall, my lord. Miss Winter awaits you. No improprieties shall be tolerated."

No kissing Eugie, that meant.

He could accept this as his penance if it meant the chance to spend the rest of his life with her. He inclined his head. "I will conduct myself as a gentleman."

"Or face my wrath," Winter prompted in a protective, brotherly growl.

"You have my word I shall not ravish your sister whilst you are within listening distance," some inner devil could not resist prodding the man.

Winter's brows snapped together. "Did I say you are daring earlier, Hertford? I do believe I meant you are stupid. That, perhaps even, you harbor a secret death wish."

Lady Emilia intervened, laying a staying hand on her husband's coat sleeve, which was all it required for the surly giant to calm. The besotted look he cast his wife was not lost upon Cam.

Because he well understood the sentiment.

"One quarter hour," Lady Emilia reminded him firmly. "No more."

He bowed to the both of them and then did not waste another moment in slipping through the door of the salon and finding Eugie. She was within, at the far end of the chamber, her back to him. He took a moment to admire the sweeping lines of her figure, the graceful curve of her neck, the flare of her hips outlined beneath her gown, as he approached her.

From any angle, she was stunning.

He almost did not want to speak and ruin the moment. Almost feared facing her until she turned. And *Christ*, the full effect of her loveliness was like running into a wall. Her eyes were wide, and she was pale, but her lips were as berry-red as ever.

Had it truly been only a smattering of hours since he had last kissed her? Since he had last held her in his arms? It seemed, all at once, as if an eternity had passed.

"Eugie," he said, recognizing he was already wasting precious minutes by lingering at the threshold.

"Lord Hertford." Her voice was hesitant.

He noted her use of his title. But he would not allow it to shake him. He stalked toward her, closing the distance keeping them apart.

He stopped just short of her, recognizing the compressed line of her ordinarily lush lips. "I am sorry," he said.

"Did you plan for us to be seen?" she asked, her dark eyes searching his.

"Is that what you think of me?" He studied her, noting the confusion, the sternness, and yet the tenderness of her eyes. "Do you truly believe I hold you in so little regard that I would arrange for Aylesford and a pair of gossips to witness our kiss just to entrap you into marriage?"

Her brow furrowed. "I do not know what to think, my lord. You have had me at sixes and sevens since we first danced at the welcome ball."

He knew the feeling. "Surely you know me better than that by now."

"But I scarcely know you at all," she said, her tone troubled. "I know you like gardens and libraries and that you have an estate in Lincolnshire. I know your father was a scoundrel who left you in debt. I know you are friends with that reprobate, Lord Aylesford."

He found himself smiling at her insult. "Aylesford is not a reprobate. A rake, perhaps, but not a reprobate."

Her lips tightened. "I do not trust him."

"Let him be your sister's worry," he said. "Why are we talking about Aylesford when I am attempting to ask you to be my wife?"

She stilled. "Is that what you are doing?"

"I was trying," he said, taking another step nearer so the warmth of her soft body burned into his and her gown brushed his legs. "But you suggested you do not know enough about me."

"I do not," she insisted, her chin tipping up.

He caught that chin in his thumb and forefinger, though he knew he should not touch her. That to do so was courting further ruin, and perhaps a severe drubbing by Devereaux Winter.

But to hell with it. She was *his*, Miss Eugie Winter, and he would not stop until she realized it too. "What do you want to know about me?" he asked.

Her tongue flicked over her lower lip, and it required every last speck of his restraint to keep from chasing it with his. "What do you like to eat?"

"You."

She colored furiously. "For dinner."

"You," he repeated softly. "And for dessert. Breakfast. With afternoon tea. You are all I want, Eugie Winter."

"My dowry," she corrected, still flushing. "My fortune is all you want."

"No." He cupped her face now, admiring the elegance of her bone structure, the silken smoothness of her skin. "Only you. I have spoken with your brother, and he has informed me of the stipulations. I have agreed I will receive no dowry. No fortune. Not a shilling until the birth of our first child, should your brother allow it."

The furrow returned to her brow. "What?"

"We shall have to make some sacrifices," he told her. "I will not be capable of giving you the life to which you have become accustomed. I was already in the process of deciding which estates must be sold to save the entail. But we shall manage. You will still have your white roses in Lincolnshire, if you will but have me as well."

"You promised me red ones too," she said.

"To match your sweet lips," he agreed. "So I did, and those, too, you shall have."

"You do not want my fortune." Eugie's hand closed over his, and she moved nearer. A half step. Their lips were almost touching.

"All I want is you," he said. And it was true. His plans for marrying a fortune to save himself from ruin were done. There was only one woman he could wed. One woman he loved. He would sacrifice everything else he had, if only he could have her.

"Me," she repeated, her voice hushed, tinged with wonder.

"You." He paused, knowing he needed to reveal himself

to her completely. "But I must make a confession to you now. Two, actually."

She raised a brow, watching him with an indecipherable expression. "What is your confession?"

"First is that I knew about your plan," he admitted. "I was on the second floor of the library and overheard you speaking with your sister. I knew you were determined to kiss Lord Ashley, and that is why I followed you the day I kissed you in the writing room. I could not bear the thought of anyone else having your kisses. Because they are mine."

"You scoundrel," she accused without heat. "I knew I heard the floor creaking that day."

He rushed on, determined he must make his second confession, which was far more damning than the first. "And the other thing I must tell you is that I love you, Eugie. You stole my heart, and it is yours now. Yours to keep forever. Will you marry me?"

HE LOVED HER.

Eugie was frozen, a violent burst of joy holding her suspended in the moment, unable to move. Unable to speak. She could do nothing but look up at his handsome face through eyes made hazy by the sudden prick of tears.

Cam loved her.

Follow your heart, Emilia had urged her.

And she felt that heart now, felt it beating in her chest, felt it swelling and filling with hope. Felt the bitterness which had dwelled inside her falling away. Felt the truth of his words deep within her. It was there, in the tenderness in his face, in the look in his eye, in the gentle way he touched her, as if she were precious. And, *oh*, that look. He looked at her as if she were beloved to him.

He was willing to give up her fortune. She was certain Dev had told him those things to test him. That Dev would not withhold her dowry. That Cam would not be required to sell off his estates.

But she would worry about all that later. For now, all she cared about was the brutal honesty of such a gesture. Her doubts fled, like rain clouds chased by the sun. And in their wake, the sky was glorious. Everything was brighter. So much brighter than she had imagined possible.

"There is something I must tell you," she said at last.

He frowned. "Eugie, let me make this right. Let me fix the wrongs I have done to you. You do not need to love me back. I love you enough for the both of us. But please, do not deny me. I cannot fathom my life without you in it."

"Cam," she began, but he pressed his thumb over her lips, stilling them when she would have continued.

"Hush," he said. "I know you do not want to marry me. I know you do not trust me, and I cannot blame you. Lord knows I have not acted the part of the gentleman since I have met you. I have been selfish and greedy, and I have not given a thought for your reputation. But I can make amends. Aylesford is my friend. He will make certain his mother says nothing, and the marchioness will be silenced as long as we wed. This scandal does not need to happen. All you have to do is say *yes*."

She could not quell the smile curving her lips behind his thumb. "Cam."

His thumb was rubbing over her lower lip slowly, languorously. "Eugie, I beg you."

Warmth flickered to life, pooling in the form of molten desire between her thighs. Just his touch brushing over her mouth. Just his nearness. His scent flitting over her. That was all it required.

"I love you," she said against the fleshy pad of his thumb.

He stiffened. "I beg your pardon?"

"I love you," she repeated. "It is just as well that I stole your heart the night of the welcome ball, because you thieved mine then too. We can take care of each other's hearts now. Because I have decided there is nothing I would like more than to be your wife."

"You do? You will?" His grin was breathtaking. He was gorgeous.

And then his lips were on hers. The kiss was hard and fast, one of possession but also one of discovery. "I will," she said into his mouth. "And I do."

"Thank God," he said on a sigh, and then she was in his arms in truth.

They were around her, surrounding her, closing over her with such tight strength. And she clutched him back with just as much need. They kissed and kissed, smiling as they did it, and then Eugie's feet left the carpet.

They were moving in a circle. For a heady moment, she actually believed her happiness had given her the delusion of weightlessness, but then she opened her eyes and realized Cam was spinning them. Their gazes locked, their mouths fused.

When he slowed them to a stop and returned her feet to the Aubusson, they swayed together, grinning at each other like drunken fools.

"If you were insistent upon that damned cottage of yours, I was going to find you there," he growled then. "Because you are meant to be mine, Eugie Winter."

"I am not certain I will be a good enough wife for the Prince of Proper," she said against a sudden fear of inadequacy. "My reputation is darkened with scandal. And I have been known to act recklessly beneath the mistletoe with the Earl of

Hertford."

"You are the perfect wife for me," he reassured her solemnly. "And together, we will restore your reputation. You will sit society on its arse."

"Are you certain?" She studied him, worrying. This was still so new, so strange.

"I have never been more sure of anything in my life, darling," Cam said. "There is but one more thing, however."

She looked up into his beautiful face, love for him radiating through her. "What is it?"

He grinned back at her. "I insist you act recklessly with me as often as possible. Mistletoe is not a requirement."

Epilogue

*T*HERE WAS ONE sight Cam loved more than his wife lingering beneath the mistletoe, he decided, and it was Eugie on her knees, those luscious red lips he could not get enough of wrapped around his cock. The Countess of Hertford was going to kill him with pleasure before she was through, he was certain of it.

But damn, what a way to die.

"Eugie," he said on a groan, his hands finding their way into the silken strands of her hair.

He intended to tell her to stop.

To carry her to the bed and take his turn ravishing her with nothing but his lips and tongue. But his wife's mouth was driving him to the brink of sanity. And when she hummed with satisfaction and took him deeper, he felt the sinful vibration of that sound in his ballocks.

He was helpless to do anything but grasp handfuls of her mahogany curls and push farther into the warm, wet depths of her heat. One of her hands gripped him at the root, and the other was caressing his thigh, her nails digging into his bare skin with almost painful pleasure.

"Damn it, wife," he gritted, surging into her mouth again, this time reaching her throat.

She withdrew and settled back on her heels, looking up at him with her slick red lips as his erect cock stood between them, shiny from her saliva, a bead of moisture leaking from his tip. "You do not like it?"

Damnation, what a carnal picture she presented, clad in nothing but an almost sheer night rail of silk and lace which had been cleverly designed by some enterprising *modiste* to tempt the most stoic of saints among men. Through it, he could see the hard peaks of her breasts, red as her lips, the lush globes begging for his hands. The curves he loved so well.

For a moment, he could not find the words to speak, as overwhelmed as he was by desire. They had been married for just a few months, and his hunger for her only grew with each passing day. Each hour. Each minute.

"I love it," he growled, "but this was not what I had in mind for the evening when I suggested we leave the ball early."

"Oh?" She pouted up at him in a way that never failed to make him desperate to have her. "But this is what I was thinking of, especially after what you did for me tonight."

What he had done for her was see to it that Baron Cunningham, that spineless, vile weasel of a man, apologized to her. Devereaux Winter had granted them full use of a handsome dowry upon their wedding day, and Cam had set aside a portion of it to buy up the rest of the man's vowels. He had offered complete forgiveness of them in exchange for the baron bowing and scraping to Eugie before some of the most esteemed members of the *beau monde*.

"I did not do it to bring you to your knees, my darling," he told her, the mere thought of Cunningham enough to make his cock go soft. "I did it so you could hold your head high. Higher than all the rest. Higher than those who would have given you the cut direct and scorned you, higher than those who believed the rumors and perpetuated the lies."

It was not lost upon him that once, he too, had believed

the worst of her. Until he had met her. Danced with her. Been charmed by her in a garden. And a library. And a darkened hall.

Until he had come to realize there was something far more precious than being the Prince of Proper, and that was being the man who loved Eugie. Full stop.

"I already held my head high before tonight," she said softly, and then, she ran the tip of her tongue down the length of his shaft. "I held my head high because I am your wife. Because you made me realize I was stronger than I knew and braver too. You made me realize I could be more than a scandal. More than a darkened reputation."

He cupped her beloved face. "You are the strongest, bravest woman I know. The way you faced them all tonight was nothing short of marvelous."

"I was ready for them." She smiled slyly, giving his prick a slow and steady stroke with her hand. "I had you at my side, and I knew none of them were any match for us."

Tonight's ball had been the official beginning of the Season. And it had marked the arrival of the Countess of Hertford in society. She was no longer a merchant's daughter, whispered about and scorned, excluded from the most fashionable society invitations. Now, she was sought after. He had seen the way everyone had watched her this evening. Everything from her gown to her hairstyle would be copied.

He had no doubt she would be the talk of Town, but for an entirely different reason than she had previously been. And he could not be more proud of her, nor happier for her than he had been the moment she had stared down the baron and given him the cut following his apology.

"You are the Princess of Proper now," he told her, enjoying the disparity between the impeccable countess she had been at the ball this evening, above reproach, and the way she looked now, tousled and flushed on the floor before him.

He found it thrilling, actually. And he wanted more. *Bloody hell*, he would take her to a dozen balls and force Cunningham into a hundred more apologies if this was the response it garnered him.

"I am afraid the Princess of Proper is about to get very, very improper. You do not mind, do you?" Her tongue found the slit at the tip of his cock, licking over it. "Mmm. I like the way you taste, husband."

Just like that, he was hard again. Ready. *Dear God*, this woman was meant to be his, and there was no question of that. He half-suspected she had to but lick him one more time, and he would spend.

He bit down on his lip to rein in his enthusiasm. "The baron did not get what he deserved. Not by half."

If Cam had been the sole deciding factor in the matter, Cunningham would have been horsewhipped. How badly he had wanted to answer for the pain she had been dealt with force, with his fists, by any means necessary. But Eugie had been the voice of reason. She had forbade violence. And so, he had settled upon the apology and the baron's public humiliation instead.

"But I got what I deserve," she whispered, her expression turning positively wicked. "And that is what matters the most."

She took him into her mouth once more, sucking and sighing and bringing him to the back of her throat. Then down it. White-hot pleasure seared him, and he had to grab the post of his bed to keep from stumbling beneath the force.

Words were streaming from his mouth, but he did not know what they were. They could have been epithets or declarations of love. His ballocks tightened, and he was going to spend in her pretty mouth, and she was going to swallow his seed.

But that was not how he wanted to end this evening.

Mustering his control, he grasped her hair and tugged until she released him with a wet, lusty pop. Her eyes were glazed, her lips slack, her chest heaving, as she looked up at him. "What is it, Cam?"

"Not this way," he managed to say, before taking her in a gentle grasp and hauling her to her feet before taking her in his arms.

Who would have thought that attending a country house party one Christmas would change his life forever? He most certainly had not. But he was grateful for the chance he had taken. Grateful for the woman in his arms.

And he was about to show her just how much.

HOW MUCH DID she love this man?

Eugie could not say. The way she felt for him eclipsed every other emotion she had ever known. She had wanted to show him with actions tonight in a way words could not convey, to worship him. To show him how beautiful he was to her: his body, his pleasure, his ceaseless championing of her. Just everything.

Every little thing about him.

The way he laughed. The way he smiled. The fringe of his lashes. The ruffled tufts of his hair in the morning. How he looked upon her as if she were the sun and the moon, all at once, in his sky.

Oh, how she loved him.

He was kissing her now, holding her as if she were necessary. Breathing her in with slow and steady inhalations, devouring her mouth which was slick with his essence.

Their tongues met.

Their hands were everywhere, traveling over each other's bodies. Each time with him was familiar and yet new. They were still learning, still finding new ways to tempt and torment and please. Still whispering secrets in the dark of the night.

He had taught her so much, not just how to love but how to trust. How to believe, blindly, in the goodness and caring of another. To believe him when he said he loved her. To accept him when he said he wanted her for the woman she was rather than the coin she had ultimately brought into their union anyway.

When she had been laid low by betrayal, embittered and wary of everyone around her, he had come into her life and shown her the power of faith. Faith in him. Faith in herself. Faith in their love.

Her night rail was gone. And the robe he had worn parted for her ministrations had been long shrugged away as they tumbled to his bed together. Eugie was on her back, her legs open, body cradling his. Their mouths clung in a passionate kiss before he broke free to rain more kisses upon her feverish flesh. Her throat. Her ear. Her shoulder, where his teeth delivered a delicious little nip.

He lingered on her breasts, toying with her nipples with his knowing fingers before lowering his head to suck one pebbled bud into his mouth. Molten honey sang through her veins, pooling in her cunny where she wanted him most.

But how delicious, his mouth upon her, suckling. Her fingers found their way into his hair, which she loved to touch. How soft it was, how full and thick.

He swirled his tongue around her nipple, making her back arch. "Such a beautiful shade of red, your nipples. Light, like a raspberry, not quite as dark as your lips. I want roses in this shade at Lyndhurst House. Along with the red and the white."

All she could do was agree when her husband's greedy mouth was sucking her nipples as if he were ravenous for her. "Yes."

He worked his way down her belly, kissing as he went, until at last his large hands settled upon her inner thighs, spreading her open for him. Once, she would have been horridly ashamed of such a display, but she had been married to him long enough to know the pleasure to be had from such intimacies. They were far more immense than he had introduced her to that first night.

He was staring at her now, his breath hot and humid upon her flesh. She was wet for him, her sex soaked, and she knew it. So did he. The intensity of his expression told her.

"And then I want some pink roses, darling." He lowered his head and licked her slit. "Pink to match your perfect cunny."

Just one swipe of his tongue over her, and she was desperate. She bowed from the bed, urging him on in a wordless plea.

A plea he accepted as he warmed to his cause, licking deeper, running his tongue through her folds. He found her pearl with unerring dedication, sucking her into his mouth in the same fashion he had her nipples. And then he moved back to her channel, his tongue sinking inside her, again and again. He hummed his appreciation as he stroked her, working her into a fine frenzy.

By the time he returned to the sensitive bud of her sex, she was mindless. He raked his teeth over her, and she reached her crescendo. Pleasure exploded, so ferocious and sudden, the spasms rocking her body bordered on painful. She came undone beneath him, and the clever lashings of his tongue prolonged it, making quakes roll through her long after the initial, violent burst had subsided.

He moved back up her body, burying his face in her neck. Reaching between them, he aligned his cock with her entrance, and in one swift thrust, he was inside her. He remained where he was, and then he withdrew, only to slide into her again. And again.

Somehow, her legs wound up against his chest, her knees hooked over his shoulders, and he was as deep as he had ever been. The rhythm he began had her crying out wildly, forgetting all about the possibility of anyone overhearing them.

"Do you like when I fuck you, Lady Hertford?" he asked.

The naughty words combined with the angle of his thrusts rendered her helpless. She reached her pinnacle again, shuddering as her sheath constricted on him so tightly she almost squeezed him from her body.

"You did not answer me, my lady," he growled, pumping his hips faster as she came beneath him. "Do you like when I fuck you?"

"Yes," she cried out, her nails raking down his broad back as yet another wave of pleasure slammed down upon her.

"Come again for me, my love," he demanded, thrusting harder.

And she did. She came, spending with such violence, her ears roared and the world turned white until the pleasure showed her mercy and began to subside into delicious ebbs. He stiffened, crying out as he spent inside her, and she knew the warm, hot rush of his seed.

He collapsed against her, his breathing as harsh as hers. "I am not hurting you, am I, darling?" he managed to ask.

The weight of him was divine. "Never." She clutched him to her tightly, relishing the feeling of him so near.

"One of these days, I hope to put my babe inside you, and

then I shall have to take greater care," he said, still breathless.

She had been caressing his shoulders, loving the hard, sinewy smoothness of them, but now she stopped. "There is something I wanted to discuss with you this evening, but then the ball and Cunningham happened, and I was distracted."

He tensed, raising his head to look down at her. "What is it that you want to discuss?"

She took a deep, bracing breath. "I believe you have."

"I have what, wife?" He frowned. "Cease speaking in riddles."

"You have put your babe inside me," she elaborated. "I have missed my courses."

"You have? You are?" He scrambled to his side, but still held her to him. "When? How long?"

"I am a month late," she told him softly, a new warmth blossoming inside her. A new sort of hope. A new sort of love. "I wanted to wait until I was certain."

"Bloody hell, woman, why did you not say something sooner?" he thundered. "I could have injured you just now. Or caused damage to the babe."

"I am well," she reassured him, smiling. "You cannot hurt me. Or the babe."

"A babe," he repeated, awe in his voice. "Our babe, Eugie."

"Ours," she agreed, feeling as if she wanted to laugh and weep all at once. "You are pleased?"

"Beyond pleased," he hastened to say, kissing her swiftly. "There is nothing I want more."

"Good," she said, kissing him again as a new wickedness flared to life. "Because there is nothing I want more either. But for the moment, I shall settle for something else."

She kissed his neck, then his chest.

"Eugie," he protested weakly. "What do you think you are

you doing?"

"You did tell me to act recklessly as often as possible," she pointed out, not the slightest bit repentant as she kissed her way down the muscles of his abdomen.

He sighed, his hand settling back into her hair. "I did, didn't I, my love?"

"You did," she agreed. "And as the woman who loves you, I have no choice but to comply."

When she made it back to the prize she had been seeking and kissed the tip of him, he was thickening once more.

"I suppose as the man who loves you, I have no choice but to allow you to have your wicked way with me, Countess." His voice was velvet and whisky, laden with anticipation and weighed down with desire.

"No choice at all," she agreed, before licking the underside of his shaft. "And you must know I am the Winter with the most wicked reputation of all."

His fingers sifted through her hair. "You are, are you? Just how wicked?"

She swirled her tongue around the head of him. "This wicked."

"That is *very* wicked indeed, my lady," he said, a smile in his voice. "I find I quite like it."

She hummed her approval. "As do I, my lord."

Then, the Prince of Proper indulged in another blissful round with his princess, but there was nothing proper about it at all, and neither one of them minded a bit.

THE END.

Dear Reader,

Thank you for reading *Wanton in Winter*! I hope you enjoyed this third book in my The Wicked Winters series and that you loved reading Cam and Eugie's story as much as I loved writing it. Their happily ever after is one of my favorite kinds, with love, laughter, and a whole lot of steam.

As always, please consider leaving an honest review of *Wanton in Winter*. Reviews are greatly appreciated! If you'd like to keep up to date with my latest releases and series news, sign up for my newsletter here or follow me on Amazon or BookBub. Join my reader's group on Facebook for bonus content, early excerpts, giveaways, and more.

If you'd like a preview of *Willful in Winter*, Book Four in The Wicked Winters, featuring the rakish Viscount Aylesford and the headstrong Grace Winter, who's about to bring him down a peg or two, do read on. And as a bonus, you can find Aylesford's sister's story in *Wishes in Winter* in the collection *A Lady's Christmas Rake*.

Until next time,

Scarlett

Willful in Winter

By
Scarlett Scott

Rand, Viscount Aylesford, needs a fiancée, and he needs one now. His requirements are concise: she must not embarrass him, and she must understand he has no intention of ever marrying her.

Miss Grace Winter is the most stubborn of the notorious Wicked Winters. When her brother decrees she must marry well, she is every bit as determined to avoid becoming a nobleman's wife. She would *never* marry a lord, especially not one as arrogant and insufferable as Aylesford.

But pretending is another matter entirely. She has to admit the viscount's idea of a feigned betrothal between them would not be without its merits. Until Aylesford kisses her, and to her dismay, she *likes* it.

Soon, their mutually beneficial pretense blossoms into something far more dangerous to both their hearts…

Chapter One

Oxfordshire, 1813

"WHILE YOUR OFFER is tempting, I must regretfully decline, my lord."

Surely Miss Grace Winter, undeniably the most stubborn chit Rand had ever met, had not just turned down his proposal. *No* female had ever turned down a proposal he had made.

Ever.

Granted, his proposals were ordinarily of a far seedier nature, and the females in question were demimondaines, but still.

He must have misheard her.

"I beg your pardon, Miss Winter," he said, frowning at her from where he stood in the Abingdon House library, "but I do believe I mistook your acceptance for a rejection."

She sighed, almost as if she found him tedious. "You did not mistake anything, Lord Aylesford. I told you no."

He frowned at her. "Women do not tell me no."

Miss Winter's lips twitched. "On the contrary, I stand before you as evidence they do."

Her lips were soft and full and the most maddening shade of pink. Every time he stared at them, he wondered if her nipples matched. But now, that mouth was laughing at him.

Laughing at his proposal.

Mocking him.

The daring of the chit was not to be borne. He ought to kiss her, he thought. Or turn her over his knee and spank her delectable rump. But he would do neither of those things. Because she was an innocent, virginal miss, decidedly not the sort of lady he preferred. And she was denying him.

"Why will you not agree to be my feigned betrothed?" he bit out.

"Because you are a rake," she said. "And one with an insufferable sense of his own consequence. If I am to be your betrothed, even your *feigned* betrothed, I will be required to spend time in your presence. To dance with you, to pretend as if I find your sallies amusing, that sort of nonsense. I would rather read a book, to be perfectly honest."

The devil.

She thought he was a rake.

Well, to be fair, he was. He had earned his reputation—that nothing in skirts was safe from him—the delicious way. He had bedded more women than he had bothered to count. The list of his conquests was longer than the Thames.

But she found him conceited? She did not want to dance with him?

"What is wrong with my sallies?" he demanded. "Why would you need to *pretend* to find them amusing?"

He was vastly amusing. All the ladies in his acquaintance told him so. They laughed at his every quip. Quite uproariously.

"I am making an assumption, of course," she said, waving a dismissive hand through the air, rather in the fashion of one chasing a bothersome fly. "I have never heard you tell one. But you do not look like the sort of gentleman who would tell clever sallies. You look like the sort who expects everyone around him to be easily wooed by his face and form."

Here, now. The baggage was not truly suggesting there was something amiss with his face? With his form? He engaged in sport whenever he could—riding, boxing, fencing, rowing. He was lean and tall. His muscles were well-honed from his exertions. And as for his face? Why, he was widely considered one of the most handsome men in London.

"I do not *expect* them to, Miss Winter," he informed her, his voice frosty with indignation for the series of insults she had paid him. "They *are* wooed by my face and form. With good reason."

She cast a dubious glance over him. "Your face and form are acceptable, I suppose. If one does not mind dark hair and blue eyes. I have always preferred blond hair and brown eyes, myself. There is something so delightful about the combination. And you are a bit thin, my lord. You might consider eating pie more often."

His face and form were *acceptable?* She was bamming him. She had to be.

He scowled at the impertinent chit, and in all his ire, he could only seem to manage one word. "Pie."

"Yes." She smiled sweetly. "Any pie you like. Consuming sweets ought to help you appear more substantial and far less gaunt, over time."

Rand had been careful to maintain a respectable distance between them for propriety's sake, even if the hour was late and there was nothing at all proper about arranging for a clandestine meeting with the unwed sister of his host. But he was not accustomed to doing anything the proper way. He was a scapegrace, it was true, and besides, everyone knew the rules of London eased at country house parties.

Did they not?

He decided they did. They had to. Especially when a man was as desperate as he was. And as irritated.

"Pie," he repeated, stalking toward her. "You recommend I eat pie, Miss Winter?"

She stiffened as he neared her, but she did not retreat, and nor did her goading smile fade. "I do, Lord Aylesford."

He stopped only when he was close enough for her gown to billow against his breeches. Her green eyes flared, and he noted the flecks of gray and gold in their vibrant depths. At this proximity, in the warm glow of the lone candle brace illuminating them, her auburn locks seemed as if they were aflame. And damn her, she was beautiful in an unconventional way. Tempting. Need roared to life inside him, sending an arrow of lust straight to his hardening cock.

"I am not hungry for pie," he told her softly.

And now, he was forgetting all the reasons he must maintain his distance. Forgetting he could not afford to compromise her if he wanted to remain unshackled by the parson's mousetrap. Forgetting he wanted her to agree to become his feigned betrothed, and that none of this—the way he had been courting her at the house party, the way he felt now—was real.

Think of Tyre Abbey, he reminded himself. The wealthy Scottish estate would be his upon his betrothal, thanks to his grandmother, the dowager duchess' stipulation. He would convince Miss Winter to agree to his plan one way or another.

He had to.

"What are you hungry for then, my lord?" she returned, her gaze dipping to his lips.

His honed rake's instincts told him Miss Grace Winter was not as unaffected by him as she pretended. Not if the way her lips had parted, the sudden huskiness in her tone, and the manner in which she had swayed toward him just now were any indication.

Perhaps the means to convince her of the wisdom of his

plan was not words at all.

"You," he said, and then he drew her soft body against his.

Want more? Look for Rand and Grace's story, *Willful in Winter*!

Don't miss Scarlett's other romances!
(Listed by Series)

Complete Book List
scarlettscottauthor.com/books

HISTORICAL ROMANCE

Heart's Temptation
A Mad Passion (Book One)
Rebel Love (Book Two)
Reckless Need (Book Three)
Sweet Scandal (Book Four)
Restless Rake (Book Five)
Darling Duke (Book Six)
The Night Before Scandal (Book Seven)

Wicked Husbands
Her Errant Earl (Book One)
Her Lovestruck Lord (Book Two)
Her Reformed Rake (Book Three)
Her Deceptive Duke (Book Four)

League of Dukes
Nobody's Duke (Book One)
Heartless Duke (Book Two)
Dangerous Duke (Book Three)
Shameless Duke (Book Four)
Scandalous Duke (Book Five)

Sins and Scoundrels

Duke of Depravity (Book One)
Prince of Persuasion (Book Two)
Marquess of Mayhem (Book Three)
Earl of Every Sin (Book Four)

The Wicked Winters
Wicked in Winter (Book One)
Wedded in Winter (Book Two) ~ Available in the special,
limited edition box set *Once Upon A Christmas Wedding*
Wanton in Winter (Book Three)
Wishes in Winter (Book 3.5) ~ Available in *A Lady's Christmas
Rake*
Willful in Winter (Book Four)
Wagered in Winter (Book Five)
Wild in Winter (Book Six)

Stand-alone Novella
Lord of Pirates

CONTEMPORARY ROMANCE

Love's Second Chance
Reprieve (Book One)
Perfect Persuasion (Book Two)
Win My Love (Book Three)

Coastal Heat
Loved Up (Book One)

About the Author

USA Today and Amazon bestselling author Scarlett Scott writes steamy Victorian and Regency romance with strong, intelligent heroines and sexy alpha heroes. She lives in Pennsylvania with her Canadian husband, adorable identical twins, and one TV-loving dog.

A self-professed literary junkie and nerd, she loves reading anything, but especially romance novels, poetry, and Middle English verse. Catch up with her on her website www.scarlettscottauthor.com. Hearing from readers never fails to make her day.

Scarlett's complete book list and information about upcoming releases can be found at www.scarlettscottauthor.com.

Connect with Scarlett! You can find her here:
Join Scarlett Scott's reader's group on Facebook for early
excerpts, giveaways, and a whole lot of fun!
Sign up for her newsletter here.
scarlettscottauthor.com/contact
Follow Scarlett on Amazon
Follow Scarlett on BookBub
www.instagram.com/scarlettscottauthor
www.twitter.com/scarscoromance
www.pinterest.com/scarlettscott
www.facebook.com/AuthorScarlettScott
Join the Historical Harlots on Facebook

Made in the USA
Monee, IL
13 April 2020